President Blog

PRESIDENT BLOG

Doug Magee

Reel Lies Books
New York, N.Y.

...and all the noisy muddle of political activity
which used to be our minor national industry and is
now our national amateur pastime.

William Faulkner — *Intruder in The Dust*

1

Eight weeks before he found himself throwing up a Subway turkey club in his hotel room at the Radisson in Concord, New Hampshire, Gary King had taken a half hour off from a strenuous Sunday watching football on TV and penned an essay that now threatened to alter the course of politics in America forever. All he was really trying to do was impress his girlfriend, Amanda, and convince her that his then current job hiatus wasn't going to be permanent.

"I don't want any presents," she had answered to his half-hearted what-would-you-like-for-Christmas mumble as he was concentrating on a red zone third down. "I want you to get back to work."

At halftime he had peeled himself off the couch, gone to his laptop, noodled around looking at new-model vape pens online, and, due to a typing error, landed on a plain-vanilla, anonymously-written blog called Common 2 Cents. He wasn't stoned but perhaps the coincidence of the vape pen search and the blog triggered an aha moment and before the second half kick-off he had come up with something tongue-in cheek he thought his friend John McKensie at Poli-Ticks might publish. He'd get the usual fifty bucks for it, but he would be able to argue to Amanda that he was working again.

"What if a candidate for president were nothing more than a stunning collection of common sense Ideas?" he had begun. "What if those Ideas came to us in the form of an anonymous blog, pronouncements intended only to put forth a thought, an observation, a question, not to persuade, but being, by the very force of their ingenuity and clear-thinking, persuasive? And what if we had no picture of this candidate, no face to face, no ads, no PACS or moneyed backers, no sense of where he or she was born, what his or her ethnic, religious, or racial makeup was, who his or her parents were, how much money he or she made, nothing, that is, but his or her Ideas? We used to talk about an idea whose time has come, and maybe that idea whose time has come should be Ideas.

"Why should you require a bodied candidate? The business-man will tell you he flies across the country and back in a day for a one-hour meeting with a potential client in order to read the client, to see the cut of his jib, to get to know him before the businessman commits to whatever scheme they're working on. A worthy goal, perhaps, and one the airlines whole-heartedly support, but of dubious value in this day and age and certainly not feasible in a presidential election. Our glimpses of the candidate's bodily appearances, even those we witness in person, are dog and pony shows intended not to reveal the true flesh and blood person but to gussie up, conceal, lead astray, and bamboozle. Yet we judge candidates on these superficialities and, worse, size them up according to how much money these dissimulations bring in to these candidates.

"Again, why do we need these bodies? Why can't we deal with Ideas? In truth there is no reason we can't. The write-in campaign has a venerable history in our country. Little used and scoffed at as a hail-Mary for losers, it nevertheless is a sleeping giant in the American political scene. FDR used it to win the New Jersey Democratic primary in 1940. Nixon and Johnson used it as well. It is a tailor-made strategy for the digital age, the highest calling perhaps for viral phenomena. Politicians today hold rallies and are

creaming their jeans when they get a stadium filled with supporters. A write-in candidate, through the force of his or her Ideas,
could rally a stadium number of supporters in fifteen minutes.
What are we waiting for?

"Well, a candidate. The beauty of what I'm talking about here
is that popularity will have a new engine. The candidate, in this
new world, might not even be interested in running for office,
but his or her Ideas are so fresh, relevant, or needed that a true
groundswell, not a phony one engineered by a PR firm, lifts this
thinker up and elects him or her.

"For instance, there's an anonymous blogger in our midst who
seems uninterested in running for office but who, should he or she
be read and liked as much as I like him or her, would be a fine candidate for the Oval Office. The blog is called Common 2 Cents
and goes by the moniker C2C and truly is a collection of very
pithy, clear-headed, indirect prescriptions for our country in this
day and age. I could easily imagine voters rallying around C2C,
spending no money on a campaign, organizing write-in campaigns via social media, and zooming C2C to the top of the presidential primaries.

"So, give it some thought. A pure candidate whose only introduction to us is his or her Ideas, supporters drawn to the candidate only because of said Ideas, the appearance of true grassroots
organizing, and the disappearance of money's influence on the
campaign. When in the course of human events it becomes necessary to, well, cast off an old system, why not do it?

"I've written this anonymously to keep to the spirit of my
thought. You don't need to know anything about me to size up
what I'm saying. Have fun. The Iowa primary is just around the
corner."

John McKensie called at the start of the fourth quarter and
said he was going to publish the piece. Gary was about to say
something about its tongue-in-cheekness when John went on for
several long sentences about what a trenchant take on the political scene it was and how he hoped Gary would support it with

interviews and such if it got any traction. Gary said he would and was once again ready to talk about the satirical bent of his essay, but John again stopped him short with, "I wasn't aware of what a fine theoretical and analytic mind you have."

Gary quoted John when he broke the news to Amanda that he was once again gainfully employed. She picked up on the essay's winks and said the piece would be the perfect Christmas gift for her father, Sam Tompkins, a six-term Democratic Congressman from Illinois. Sex was much better that night than it ever was on a football Sunday simply by dint of its existence. Gary drifted off to sleep pleased with himself, looking forward to the new vape pen he'd ordered once he'd found out he was fifty dollars richer.

John McKensie called at noon on Monday to say that the essay had hit some sort of nerve, that it was being pinged around social media like a cute cat video and that Gary should fasten his seat belt. Gary was yet again about to mention that he wasn't really being all that serious in the piece, but John hung up quickly saying he had to "ride the galloping viral horse." Gary thought the metaphor atrocious but during the next couple of days he kept repeating it to himself as things in his life went haywire. His anonymity lasted only a few hours, John saw to that, and his notoriety went from zero to the stratosphere in no time.

As can happen with such phenomenon, it was the negative voices, the critics, the scoffers who put the flame to the fuel, denouncing the Ideas manifesto as rubbish and nonsensical and totally unworkable. The counter punch from those who took the essay seriously, which was almost the whole world, was voluminous and excited and, with the presidential primary season about to launch in a month, a welcome breath of fresh air in the interminable, dull campaign in progress.

Gary had lain low at first, certain the storm would blow out as quickly as it had blown in, but the thing had legs. When Vice-President Todd Townsend, the shoo-in Democratic candidate for president, went completely loco after being asked by a moderator in a debate about C2C, and when his poll numbers dropped overnight, Gary was forced to come out of the shadows. He tried to be honest. In an interview with Honey Wallace of NPR he sloughed off her gushing approval with some aw-shucks-I-was-just-playing-around quips, but that backfired, the blogosphere seeing him as self-effacing, homespun, and unassuming, in much the same way they saw C2C.

C2C, meanwhile, was lying even lower than Gary. A cyber manhunt was hitting dead end after dead end in the quest to unmask him or her, the blog's encryption something the world's cyber sleuths had not been able to penetrate. Gary had assumed, when the attention began building and when people started talking about a real write-in campaign, that C2C would step up, say it was he or she behind the blog and thanks, but no thanks on the candidacy, that he or she was too busy running his or her dry cleaning business or teaching kindergarten. But C2C kept quiet in the real world and published only a couple of brief but compelling posts while the phenomenon swirled. Those posts became headline events even though they made no mention of the movement to draft him or her and seemed completely unaware of what was taking the country by storm.

There were, of course, hundreds of pretenders to the throne and many thousands who were spying on neighbors and co-workers suspected of being C2C. The search became a meta phenomenon that attracted a vast array of investigators, conspiracy theorists, loonies, and geniuses, but to no avail. The punditocracy publicly hoped C2C would not be found or reveal himself or herself so that Gary's original Ideas idea might be put to the test in the primaries. The non-candidacy made many nostalgic for the brief flare-up that had been Donald Trump a few years earlier, the fun of pretending along with the candidate that he was a real contender when everyone knew he was bound to be voted off the island.

Gary hoped the Iowa caucuses would tamp down the frenzy. That quirky delegate selection process, in which people stand around in school gyms, libraries, churches, and bowling alleys, clumping with other supporters of various candidates, trying to get their neighbors to join them, the first primary-like vote in the presidential campaign, would not be friendly to C2C's insurgency, he thought, and would pop the balloon that was growing larger by the hour. But a week before the Iowa caucuses, as the announced candidates zipped around the frozen cornfields of the state, interrupting hundreds of breakfasts in diners, homemade C2C posters and yard signs became ubiquitous. The nascent, leaderless, social media-driven non-campaign even got a theme song when people began singing America The Beautiful and belting out its "From sea to shining sea" line, leaving out the "shining." After only a few days the first few bars of the song were enough to get ad hoc gatherings of C2C supporters on their feet.

Gary and Amanda debated going to Iowa for the caucuses, but because Gary didn't want any more spotlight on him than he was already getting, and because he hoped Iowa would be his little essay's demise, and, last but not least because the Super Bowl was the weekend before the primary, they decided to sit tight in Washington. Like most of his strategy in the past few weeks, that stay-at-home effort backfired as well. Commentators and C2C supporters alike interpreted Gary's reluctance to promote either himself or C2C as a sign of his purity, a confidence in his original belief that a candidate need not have a physical presence in order to be viable. In an interview he mentioned that John Ashcroft had once lost a primary to an opponent who had died a month before the voting. "Remember Ashcroft" graffiti popped up all over the country, even in the rural counties of Iowa.

Todd Townsend, who had learned his lesson after his debate explosion, adopted a studied scoff when asked about the anonymous blogger, and got some kudos for winkingly saying he didn't know who C2C was when, of course, nobody knew who C2C was. This was seen as levity coming from the dour vice-president. The other two candidates still in the Democratic race, Senator Jill Castle, a bland policy wonk whose husband was the founder and owner of the software giant MegaMeta, and Don Michaels, a multi-billionaire who had made his first pile shorting bundled mortgages during the sub-prime bubble, seemed most deeply offended by the fact that the non-campaign was raising no money, relying solely on free social media, and was outstripping their wildly expensive PR apparatuses in things like Google searches and media mentions, by a wide country mile.

A polar vortex gripped Iowa and most of the Plains states on the day of the caucuses and the sages at CNN and most other outlets predicted a smaller than usual turnout, one they said would favor the entrenched Townsend candidacy. But the turnout was large and C2C didn't suffer. Gary and Amanda, gathered with a large group of friends in an Adams-Morgan pub, were as shocked as any when the first numbers started rolling in and C2C was in second place to Townsend by only five percentage points. As the evening went on and Townsend's lead nose-dived, then vanished, as C2C, looking like a sprinter with a second wind began to pull away from the three others, as America The Beautiful seemed to be the night's theme song, and as Amanda went into the uncharted territory of a third martini, Gary felt his loosened tie become something of a noose. When the final numbers put C2C at forty percent, far ahead of the Democratic field, Gary was, he guessed, fucked.

He managed to get the wildly ecstatic Amanda out the back door of the pub and avoided the friends and media clamoring for a comment. Amanda slowed their cold walk to her apartment with a couple of martini regurgitations, but even those couldn't dampen her drunk and oft-repeated "we did it!" claims. Gary who had decided early in the evening that inebriation wasn't going to help anything, kept the stumbling Amanda vertical while he wondered how the hell he was going to get himself out of the mess he'd created.

As Amanda lay sound asleep fully dressed, Gary made a phone call he had been contemplating for a few days. Ginny Evans, a former girlfriend, a full professor at CalTech, who had recently told her Facebook friends that she was no longer interested in penises, answered immediately.

"I thought you'd be calling," she said.

"I need your help, Ginny."

"I bet you do."

"You saw the Iowa results?"

"No, Gary. I'm just a, what did you call me, lab rat? Who doesn't care a fig about politics?"

"It was in the heat of an argument. I... You know I don't feel that way."

"Well, your intemperate shouting helped me make a life-changing assessment of my own feelings, and so I suppose I have to thank you for that."

"You became a lesbian because of me?"

"Please, Gary, please. Come into the twenty-first century. If my friends knew you had just asked me such a moronic question and I hadn't immediately hung up, I could be in serious trouble. Let's get to the point. You need to find C2C, right?"

"Right."

"And you think that even though the entire world has been tearing up the wires trying to find the guy, and it most definitely is a guy, that I, who once was concerned to make you think I was some sort of computer geek genius, could be the only person on the planet to find him. Right?"

"Well, not the only person. But the only one I'd trust."

"You trust me?" Ginny said, obviously a little thrown by this.

"I do. And I need to know that whoever I go to to get me out of this jam will keep things quiet, at least until we find out who C2C is."

"Why would you think I'd keep quiet?"

"Because deep down you like me. You liked me back then and you like me now. You wouldn't have taken my call if you didn't."

"Your naiveté is charming. But in this case you're probably right. I can keep quiet. I certainly don't want to be associated with the founder and chief bottle washer of this C2C nonsense."

"You think it's nonsense?"

"I do."

"So you'd like to help put it out of its misery, right?"

"Theoretically, yes. But I have even more of a need for privacy in this than you do."

"I would promise complete privacy."

"Are you calling me on an encrypted line?"

"Uh, encrypted line? Phone line? Encrypted? I thought…"

"Right. Thanks for illustrating my point. Anyway, I don't think I could help you no matter what."

"But you were right back then. You are a genius."

"There's a word that should be retired. Gary, my area of expertise is quantum decoherence and lattice vibrations, which has about as much to do with ferreting a IP address from a transistor based system as, I don't know, running a bogus campaign for a non-candidate."

"That's not strictly true. Quantum decoherence is a disruption in the computational abilities of a system due to interference from outside the system. There must be transistor based parallels that could open possibilities for disruption of the encryption."

Ginny was quiet for a few seconds. "You listened," she said finally.

"You were a good teacher."

"Maybe, but I still don't traffic in cyber sleuthing. I've got plenty of friends who do, however, and I know most of them have taken a look at the C2C situation and would love nothing more than to work with the genius who kicked over the whole bucket of shit in the beginning."

"But I wouldn't be able to trust them."

"But they might get you where you want to go."

Now it was Gary's turn for a little silence. "I wish I knew where I wanted to go. I thought I'd be on a one-way ride to Palookaville by now and I could get back to the playoffs and pot and generally not living up to my potential. I don't know if I want C2C to be revealed or not. But I would like to know who he or she is before I make that decision. I have nightmares about C2C being a child pornographer. I have nightmares about C2C being one of the most humane, funny, and intelligent examples of the species ever sculpted. I'm desperate."

"I'd say you're more like an idiot savant."

"Thank you, for half of that."

"You did say something about disrupting the encryption, didn't you?"

"A yeah, but, confession, I was just dragging up whatever I could remember from what you…"

"But." Ginny seemed lost in thought. "I'll call you back tomorrow as long as you encrypt your line before then."

"How do I do that?"

"You'll figure it out. Somehow your limited brain is turning politics in America inside out. You can find out how to encrypt a phone."

Ginny, with many caveats, agreed the next day to help Gary, but she hadn't struck gold a week later when they talked and Gary was getting very nervous about the New Hampshire primary, which was looming. There had been no posts on the C2C blog and the media, literally and figuratively, knocked on Gary's door most of the day and night. Employers too besieged Gary with very attractive job offers, ones Gary kept seeing as transparent attempts to cozy up to the story of the moment, ones that would probably disappear like mist once C2C came out of the woods. A circle of real friends, not Facebook ghosts but the kind you could watch a game with, the kind you could trust not to give out your newly encrypted phone number, coalesced and became a de facto campaign committee, though Gary insisted that there was no campaign committee.

Gary wished his parents were available to be on the ad hoc committee but they were quite literally off the grid. Both were ethnographers who had been superb parents to their only child. They taught at SUNY Buffalo, attended all Gary's games and events, and waited until he was out of the house to follow their own dreams. They were now embedded in a nomadic tribe in Mongolia and had, by their own wish for authenticity, no modern communication tools at all. In an extreme emergency Gary had the number of a villager a hundred miles from them who could get a message through. But Gary hadn't used that pony express yet. He was a bit sad they were most likely unaware of all the hubbub.

The non-campaign committee made plans to be in New Hampshire for the primary, but Gary had his reservations. He and Amanda once again debated whether they should be on site for the vote, but this time Amanda was firmly in the go camp. When she came out of the shower one night, sans robe, her body pink and soft and glowing, Gary accused her of trying to influence his decision with her wiles and she copped to the attempt. It worked however and a week later they arrived at the Radisson in Concord, Gary's presence a magnet for the media.

Gary's meager responses and limited time in front of the cameras was thin gruel for the raucous international press corps charging around the state, and so they turned their attention to experts and the other candidates and anyone who was willing to do anything other than sing America The Beautiful. Gary thought he detected a backlash, a sense in the media, in the populace, that the jig was up, that the country was finally catching on to his satire. But then on the weekend before the Tuesday primary things got seriously weird. A spontaneous, social media-fueled caravan of what was estimated to be over eleven thousand cars flooded the major arteries of the state. I-93, the route from Boston to Concord, was backed up Woodstock-style for forty miles, and a giant C2C party engulfed the major cities and towns. The very gyms and public spaces that would hold the voting stations became crash pads for those thousands who couldn't be accommodated by the state's hotels, motels, and bed and breakfasts. After being forced out of a Denny's on Sunday morning because of a crush of C2C supporters and reporters eager to get his every word on tape, Gary, with Amanda and his cohort, retreated to the Radisson and holed up there for the duration.

On Tuesday morning Gary woke up with a pounding headache, the result of going hard liquor the night before, and looked out the hotel room window. A brilliant blue sky and blazing banks of snow amped his headache. He squinted and saw what looked like a giant caterpillar snaking it's way toward the hotel. He waited for his brain to process what he was seeing and soon realized it was a line dance of C2C supporters, several blocks long, headed his way. Amanda got up and stood beside him watching the scene.

"Wow," she said.

"Yeah," Gary grunted. "Where's the Advil?"

Gary went to the bathroom while Amanda continued to look out. When he returned the crowd was beginning to fill the circular drive in front of the hotel and two police cars, lights atwirl were arriving.

"You're going to have to say something to them, Gary," Amanda said, realizing at the same time that she was standing in front of the window naked. She went for the plush hotel robe.

"What am I going to say?"

"Thank them for coming out in the fucking cold."

"Thank them?"

"They're fulfilling your wish."

"My wish? I was just..."

"Don't start that again. We're way too far down the road for that shit. I think you've got to loosen up, Gar. You didn't <u>do</u> anything, remember? You just spoke your mind. They are the ones doing stuff. Look at those signs. Jesus. Not one like another. Man."

"Well, I'm not going to say anything. Not now. If there's going to be a significant write-in vote, then I guess I'll have to say something, but not now."

"<u>If</u> there's going to be a significant write-in vote. Honey, look out there."

"But they're not all locals. Most of them probably can't vote here."

"You don't think their presence will make a difference?"

"I don't know. The polls say C2C will come in fourth."

"Come on, Gar. Those polls are dinosaurs. They still call people up on landlines. Those people out there? They don't have landlines. You want to poll them go to where they live, online.

Gary didn't reply. He started to get dressed and waited for the Advil to kick in. The hotel room began to fill up with his inner circle, the team he and Amanda had partied a little too hard with the night before. At about one o'clock they had dubbed themselves the C2Seagrams. Ed Popper, a childhood friend of Gary's from Buffalo, an offensive tackle on Gary's high school football team, was the lead partier. He had gone to USC and made the team there as a walk-on, came close to starting, then blew out his knee. He was now trying his hand at acting in L.A. and was confined so far to hulking-black-friend-of-the-bad-guy roles. His girlfriend Rhonda, a yoga instructor, had them all doing poses deep in the night. She suggested some to begin the day and got no takers. Wanda Samuels, a friend from his days slaving away for Congressman Jim Hawkins, was the only seasoned political campaigner other than Gary. She had tried to make the operation at the Radisson look like a real campaign headquarters but wasn't having a lot of luck. Mark Parish, Gary's roommate from Georgetown, a self-professed train wreck junkie, said he had to come along for the ride to see how Gary was going to get his ass handed to him. Bella Cardoza, Gary's cousin from Buffalo, and her husband Vince, said they were representing the family, but the others suspected some ulterior motive. Bella was a Facebook junkie who heretofore had been content to post cute cat videos until she hitched her wagon to the C2C juggernaut. Vince was a quiet observer who unnerved the loquacious cohort around Gary. Both were lifelong Republicans. Ginny Evans was present via Skype from California. When she saw the groaning, hungover, group she said she could almost smell the booze on their breaths. Amanda had been a bit frosty to Ginny the day before but then they realized they had a lot in common and found they often sided with each other against Gary's ideas. Gary didn't mind. Most of the time he didn't know what to think. He was happy to have the two of them be definite.

The consensus of the group was that Gary should not address the rabble before the polls closed but that he should definitely do so after, win or lose. Amanda, with Ginny's support, filed a dissent, saying those people deserved better. Gary said she was free to go talk to the crowd still milling around peacefully in front of the Radisson. Amanda, who had promised her father she wouldn't have her mug in front of the cameras, gave in.

Despite biting cold the crowd of C2C supporters remained large throughout the day and as five o'clock rolled around, the sun lipping the horizon, the temperatures dropping even farther, more and more people started to show up. From their room and from reports of those who went down to join in the festivities Gary knew that there was something good about what was going on. There wasn't an anger factor, there was no us-against-them vibe. This was hopeful. He went into the bedroom to do a vape hit. Amanda was there reading something on her phone. They shared the vape and Gary sat on the bed as if he were visiting a patient.

"I think we ought to talk about our future," Gary said.

"I think we ought to talk about our future when we're not stoned in our present, and we don't have a few thousand people outside our window," Amanda replied.

Gary nodded. "Yeah. Another time. This is pretty weird, isn't it, all those people?"

"Good weird."

"Is there such a thing?"

"I don't know. We'll figure that one out when we're in our rockers."

"When we're in our rockers? Like, you and me, sunsets?"

"We'll see." Amanda leaned over and pulled Gary into a kiss. "We've got a way to go before all that."

As the polls closed Gary's room was lit almost entirely by the TV screen and multiple laptops. The brain trust were all looking at different outlets and trying to relay information to others, but Gary thought it looked a little too sci-fi-ish for his liking. He was getting very antsy. He and Amanda had tried to write something for him to say, but it all sounded wooden.

"Be true to your philosophy, Gar," she had said at last.

"How's that?"

"Wing it. Go out there and speak the truth."

"Which is?"

"Good question. The truth of the moment. What you feel, what you think. And you've got to remember that it doesn't mean anything."

"What doesn't mean anything?"

"The vote. The primary. All this activity and people in the streets. We're like dogs given a little extra leash right now. C2C wins this, or even makes a strong showing and there will be a glut of lawyers, very expensive lawyers paid for by very rich people who will proceed to shut down the whole stunt. So, live it up, you know?"

Gary knew she was right, but he didn't like the downbeat tone. All those expensive lawyers would be playing by old rules. Things are changing. Just look at the way C2C came together. Who knows what might happen?

The local Subway sent up a platter of sandwiches gratis and even though he'd gone through a sizeable amount of the pizza Bella had ordered up earlier, he downed a turkey club, eyes glued to his laptop. He had most of the club down when the first numbers hit. C2C and Townsend were in the mid-thirties, the other two in the tens, which didn't add up until Gary realized they were talking about exit poll numbers. Then Mark Parish commanded everyone to go to CNN and when they did they heard Wolf Blitzer saying that results for C2C would be marked by an asterisk. Boos around the room. Then the brain trust oohed and aahed as the first real numbers came up and, surprisingly, a prediction. C2C, with forty-one percent of the votes counted already, had a thirty-nine to twenty-nine percent of the vote lead over Townsend and had a check mark next to the name, which CNN had spelled out.

Gary headed for the bathroom, released the turkey club, cleaned up and looked at himself in the mirror. Well, he looked in the mirror. He wasn't seeing anything but a sea of reporters, a flotilla of microphones, a blanket of ardent supporters, and his mouth and brain lockjawed. If Amanda came in again with that it-doesn't-mean-anything bullshit he was going to have to protest.

"Gary?"

"I'm okay. God. Do we have a plan B?"

Amanda came farther into the bathroom, wrinkling her nose against the smell, putting a consoling hand on Gary's shoulder. "We didn't really have a plan A, hon. But the shit here is that in about an hour or so we're going to have to go downstairs and face the music."

Gary looked at her and on cue they heard strains of America The Beautiful making it up five floors, through therma-pane glass, a living room, bedroom and a bathroom door.

"I think a little vape hit's in order," Gary said, holding Amanda's bright blue round eyes firmly in his. She blinked a couple of times.

"I'm not sure that's a good idea, Gar. There's that half an hour of paranoia for you and you wouldn't want to have that hit when you go down there."

"So, we'll time it well."

"No 'we'. I'll have to be your wingperson if you're going to do this."

"You said not to sweat it, right?"

"Yeah, but, you don't want to embarrass yourself. This whole thing could lead to significant career advancement."

"I'm just going to take a sip and figure out what I'm going to say. Help settle my stomach too. Watch."

He rummaged in his essentials baggie, found his vape pen, and took, as he had said, a sip. The blue vapor actually helped a bit with the room's sharp smells and he smiled over at a very skeptical Amanda. He started to take one more little sip but she stopped him with a gentle hand on his wrist and a look that said something like, do that and I might have to get ugly.

By the time Gary and Amanda got back to the living room of the suite, C2C's lead had increased and stood at 43 percent to Townsend's stalled 29 percent. The other two candidates were straining to break into double digits. Gary stared at the TV screen as his sip of pot took effect. The excitement in the room was bubbling all around him, but Gary latched onto the numbers on the screen and tried to make sense of them. It wasn't some sort of pot high incomprehension. It was deeper than that. He understood the numbers and even their historical significance, but he was also gripped by a sense of his own powers. Once he had read Paul McCartney's account of The Beatles' concert at Shea Stadium in their first tour of America. He remembered McCartney talking about how the bedlam made it impossible for the band to really hear what they were playing and so they were just looking at each other hoping they were in synch. Then McCartney recalled playing with the audience. He found that if he pointed the neck of his bass at one section of the crammed infield or the stands, that section would scream even louder. As the concert went on he started to sweep the bass over the crowd and watched as the screaming seemed to lift off the audience and roll as a wave might. He talked about the feeling of both power and fright he got doing this, amazed that he could command such an upheaval, frightened to think what someone with evil intent might do with such power.

And there it was on the screen for Gary. He had scribbled something one Sunday afternoon about eight weeks earlier and now here was the fruit of that, a stunning, major victory for a ghost, one he had identified and promoted. There was definitely power in that, and for a few minutes, as the hotel room buzzed and whooped, he thought he was up there on the stage in Shea Stadium raking the crowd with his bass. But the joy of the power soon gave way to its darker elements and he realized that maybe for the first time in his life he had a deep responsibility for his actions. Not that he'd been some sort of uncaring, irresponsible lout to that point, just that he hadn't had anything near the duty of throwing the country over his shoulder and leading it to a new future.

This sort of grandiosity made him realize his little sip had been quite effective and he geared down from savior of the Republic to what the fuck he was going to say about the whole thing. He found himself speaking loudly to the room.

"What is happening?!"

The ecstatic replies surprised him. He had expected the same sort of incomprehension he was feeling from his close friends but they were more like drunks in a sports bar on Super Sunday. Amanda was by his side then and he was glad to see she still had her feet on the ground.

"The people have spoken," she said.

"Isn't that what they all say when they win?" Gary asked.

"Well, they really have, haven't they?"

She had a point. Maybe what they were looking at was one of the purest iterations of democracy possible. Maybe C2C's ascendancy had poked a big hole in the way leaders are chosen in America, a hole that could never be closed now. Maybe it was Gary's job to go downstairs and lead the country through that big hole to a new morning.

"How stoned are you?" Amanda asked.

"Me? Fine. What do we do now?"

"We take the elevator downstairs and we go outside and we say something to the media while the crowd cheers us on, except for one thing. The "we" is you. And we need to know if you are up to the task."

"Of course I am."

"You just left your lunch in the bathroom."

"Florence Nightingale left her lunch in the bathroom before every performance in her life."

"Florence Nightingale was a nurse."

"I mean the other one, the opera singer, Jenny or something."

"Where did you get that one from?"

"I think my mother told me that. Anyway, I'm ready."

"What are you going to say?"

"I don't know. Wasn't it you who said I should speak from the moment? Let's see what's going on down there and I'll react to it. After all, there are no leaders in the movement, right?"

Riding a wave of pot-fueled self-confidence, Gary led most of his cohort out of the hotel room, down the elevators, past gawking onlookers, to a truly chaotic scene in the cramped lobby of the hotel. When his presence became known a surge of humans, cameras, microphones and lights rushed his way and soon had him surrounded. Outside news of his arrival set the now-huge crowd singing America The Beautiful again and alternately chanting, "Ga-ry! Ga-ry!" Ed Popper, the biggest of Gary's group, managed to keep the crowd from crushing Gary and a small phalanx of state troopers opened up an alleyway so Gary could make it outside. He hadn't planned to be outside and, dressed only in a thin shirt, felt the icy air as soon as he left the confines of the lobby.

The blast of screams and applause that greeted him was amplified by whatever it is pot does to your hearing and he thought for a few seconds he'd stepped inside a whirling jet engine. Someone put a megaphone in his hand and showed him where the trigger was. The megaphone squawked and that sent the crowd into even more frenzied activity. The media were trying to set up microphones and a makeshift podium, but the people in the front of the crowd, a line of faces that made Gary think of Norman Rockwell, made sure the media didn't get the best positions. Gary swiveled to his left, pointed the megaphone and before he got a word out, heard the scream level to his left rise. Hello Sir Paul. Gary swept the megaphone left to right and, sure enough, got a wave-like response. Very cool.

The crowd took this to be a sign and the ones in the front began shushing the ones in back and soon, miraculously, a crowd later estimated at almost a thousand people went from Beatlemania to Bach listeners in a few short seconds. Gary watched the breath puffs rise and comingle and thought what an apt symbol their coming together was. Could he make something of that? Could he relate the breath puffs to what had happened in the past two months? Could he... He forgot for a moment what he was going to connect to what and so he just opened his mouth, as Amanda had suggested, and let loose.

"Forty-three percent!" he shouted, the megaphone complaining but relaying the words clearly enough.

Shouts went up like rockets and another chorus of America The Beautiful followed. Gary, through the megaphone joined in at the "sea to (silence) sea!" In the brief moment after the singing had stopped Gary jumped in.

"Ideas rock! The voters of New Hampshire know that. You know that. There's no turning back now. On to South Carolina!"

The combination of the cold, the pot, and the energy needed to get these sentences out loudly enough to be heard in the back of the swell made Gary a little light-headed and he steadied himself against Ed Popper's pillar of a body next to him. The crowd did a minute or two of, "South Carolina! South Carolina!" and Gary managed to get his balance. Again he decided to not decide what to say, just to say it.

"I just want to say one thing and then let you go someplace warm," he said.

A shout interrupted him. "Forty-three percent has us very hot!"

The crowd went nuts at this and Gary let the hoots and hollers roll on for a long time before he cut them off.

"To those of you who voted today, C2C thanks you. To those of you who came from far away, C2C thanks you. To those of you who have stood out here all day long, C2C thanks you. You are remaking democracy. You are at the vanguard of a new America and a new world. The billionaires are not going to be happy about this. They're going to come at you tooth and nail. But hang in there. Read Common 2 Cents. Let your voices be heard. From coast to coast, from sea to a very sunny, shining sea!"

That last word was echoed by the crowd and Gary turned to go into the hotel. The state troopers weren't as good getting him back in the building as they had been getting him out. Reporters and cameramen, experienced elbowers, blocked his path and Gary heard a Babel of questions bombard his pot-tainted hearing. He ignored them and followed Ed Popper through a hole he was making the same way he had followed him through holes in high school football. Amanda was hanging on to Gary's belt and the two of them managed to get inside the lobby and were shoved into the first elevator that opened. The doors closed and they found themselves sharing the elevator with a Mom and son in swimsuits, the son shivering, the Mom wide-eyed with fear.

Amanda apologized briefly to the Mom before she and her son got off on the second floor. When the doors closed Gary's ears, still buzzing with the noise of the crowd, missed what Amanda was saying.

"What?" he said.

"What were you thinking?"

"What do you mean?"

"What you said. You said C2C thanks them."

"And?"

"And? Gary, the implication was clear. You made it seem as if you'd been in contact with C2C. Didn't you hear those questions from the reporters? You got some major 'splaining to do."

"No, that wasn't what I meant. I just meant if he or she was watching."

The doors to the elevator opened. A smiling slip of a young woman stood in front of the doors holding a microphone, a cameraman over her shoulder, his movie light blazing, angling for a shot.

"Hi, Gary. Jan Rollins, WCND. Is C2C with you now or did you talk by phone?"

Amanda led them past Jan and the cameraman without a word

and made it into their suite before any more reporters found them.

"See what I mean," Amanda said.

"I know, but I didn't..."

"Gary, honey, you've got to get real. Are you high?"

"No, not really."

"Then you've got to face it. You kicked this thing off back when and now you've kicked it into another gear. You don't want this to be about you but for now, without the real C2C, it is all about you. Is that sinking in?"

"Yes," he said, and realized that whatever was sinking in had sunk to his stomach and he was about to lose whatever was left down there. As he headed for the bathroom he managed part of a sentence.

"I didn't mean..."

2

The snow was coming sideways now, lake effect flakes big as your fist, the windshield wipers working overtime, groaning with the effort to keep some acreage on the glass clean. NPR was crackling on about the primaries in New Hampshire. Adam Malloy poked the radio's power button and let the scraping slap of the wipers be the soundtrack for a while. He didn't understand the frenzy, how something simple and straightforward had become this avalanche of voter interest. His wife Michelle was deeply involved in the hoopla. She had tried to recruit him, but he had begged off saying he was too busy with work. That was not really the truth, but close to it.

He didn't want to think about that now. He had left Boston in the afternoon, the sky clear. His goal had been to get to Buffalo that night, to set himself up in a motel there, but it didn't look like he was going to make it past Rochester. He had already slowed to what he considered a dangerously low speed and he was worried that a plow or tractor-trailer would run up his ass and shove him off the highway. He was losing sight of the road for long seconds at a time, even though he was straddling the broken white line, and he didn't want to end up in a ditch or worse.

A green and white glare emerged quickly from the snow swirl. He had just enough time to read the road sign and realize there was an exit in two miles. He decided he was going to take it even if it was one of those desolate county road exits. He'd stop for a while and let his nervous system take a break. He steered his car to the right and began to look for the curving line that would show him the off ramp. Then his headlights dug up something that wasn't snow, wasn't road sign, off to the right, a blue-black lump rushing at him. He swerved left and passed whatever it was quickly. The afterimage that came to him was of the back of a car, a figure, a man probably, sitting on the trunk. He pulled over to the right, heard the crunch of tire on gravel, slowed and stopped.

He couldn't see anything in the rearview mirror. He waited, thinking whoever it was back there would either come to him or get in his car and turn on some lights. But nothing happened, and with no other cars following him, there wasn't even a silhouette of the car and man to see. He flicked on his hazard lights, got out of the car in just his shirt, and walked back through the stinging snow to where he thought the car was.

A semi came over the rise then and sent two powerful beams into the horizontal snow. The light hit the car and the man, the truck's horn sounded through the hissing wind as it blew by, and he could see now that he was only yards away from the stopped vehicle.

"Hey! What's up?"

The snow swallowed the words and he moved forward. The car was a dilapidated Toyota or Honda or something, and as he passed it he could see that the driver's side window was open, snow dusting the interior. He moved toward the rear and repeated his question. He couldn't tell if the shadowy figure there heard. It didn't move. Suddenly a flashlight snapped on and the beam whipped through the flakes and hit him full face.

"Stay right there," a voice behind the flashlight commanded.

He stopped. The voice sounded young but its youth didn't soften its menace.

"Are you okay?" he asked.

"Get back in your vehicle and keep moving," the voice said

evenly, and he heard training in the words, as if the voice was coming from a cop or a soldier.

"Sure, but you need any help? I've got jumper..."

The shot's report was muffled by the wind and snow, but the orange lick that came from behind the flashlight and the definite pop of a handgun told Adam that whoever it was out there had just fired at something. He stood his ground.

"I said get back in your vehicle and keep moving!"

A car came over the rise then and he considered flagging it down, but he didn't want to spook whoever was behind the flashlight, didn't want to involve someone else in the situation. The car went by in the passing lane and the headlights were too weak to see the man on the car. The flashlight beam remained plastered to his face. He wiped away the snow collecting on his hair and forehead. He could barely see anything. He decided to go with a hunch.

"When did you get back?"

There was no response. But there was no gun shot either. He moved a little closer.

"I'm a doctor. If you're hurt or anything..."

The flashlight dropped a little. He took another step toward it, toward whoever was behind it. A foolish thing to do, he thought. He should be hightailing it for help. But he couldn't do that. He was only a few feet away now. The flashlight was bobbing as if it was about to drop. He reached out and took the light. He got no resistance. He turned the light around.

She had her hair up under her field cap and her features were hard, but there was no doubt she was a woman, no doubt she was in deep distress, and no doubt that his hunch had been right. She was in fatigues, the service handgun she had fired earlier was pointed at him.

"Return to your vehicle," she said again, this time through tears.

"Once we call them heroes, we put them in an untenable position," Adam wrote several hours later, after he had gotten help for the soldier and found a motel. "We have to think differently about the people we send to war. Shelve that word, hero. We send humans to war, humans protect us, and no matter what they do on the field of battle, they return as humans. We ask our soldiers to do extraordinary things, don't compound the problem by giving them an impossible label to live up to."

3

Sam Tompkins invited his daughter, Amanda, and Gary to dinner and chose an out-of-the spotlight little restaurant near his 3rd Street apartment. Gary had been getting the celebrity treatment in the week since the New Hampshire primary and Sam was afraid that some paparazzi might snap them eating together, publicity Sam did not want.

Gary and Amanda had doubts about the dinner, knowing that it wasn't just a father-daughter-boyfriend get-together. Sam had already tried several times to get Amanda to come to her senses. He had made a direct approach through a couple of phone calls, he had had Amanda's older brother, Michael, a tax attorney in Chicago, do the same, and he had recruited his current wife, Amanda's step-mother, Charlene, to give it a try. All failed and so when they got the invitation Amanda made her father promise the dinner would not have the feel of an intervention. Gary thought this was impossible, that Sam, who was prominent in the Democratic National Committee, would be obligated by his party status to try to 180 his daughter. But in the end they decided it might be better to hear the imprecations and pleadings directly, and the restaurant had five stars on Yelp.

Sam, sober for over eight years, nevertheless made sure Amanda and Gary had as much wine as they wanted and they all joked about his crude tactic. He kept insisting the dinner was just a way for him to see how things were going inside their bubble. A dapper former Marine who had left his first wife, Amanda's mother, for a much younger woman only to have her leave him for a much younger man, the cliché of all clichés, Sam was now happily settled into a second marriage and comfortably in control of his seat in Congress.

Gary was enjoying a fluffy wedge of tiramisu when Sam said he was sorry but he had to ask one question about C2C. Amanda gave him a look but he plowed ahead anyway.

"You don't have to say anything but yes or no, no identifiers or anything, but do you know the identity of C2C?"

Amanda looked at Gary. Gary looked at Sam as he let the creamy dessert sluice his throat.

"I do," he said. Amanda scowled but hoped her father hadn't picked up on that.

"You do?"

"I do."

"Then why haven't you let the rest of us know?"

"That would kind of spoil the fun, wouldn't it?" Gary said. He could see immediately that his light response, in line with the tone of the dinner so far, had been a mistake. Sam's eyes hardened and he started tapping the handle end of his knife on the table. Amanda tried to head off the inevitable follow up response.

"Not like fun fun, Dad. Not yuck it up fun. Gary meant..."

"I have a good idea what Gary meant," Sam said. "The whole country has a good idea what Gary meant. He meant that politics to him is some sort of colossal joke and now that he's gotten social media to follow him through the looking glass, he's laughing even harder."

"Whoa. Wait a minute Sam," Gary said. "When I wrote that piece in Polit-Ticks I didn't have any idea what would happen. I just wrote the piece and the rest was out of my hands."

"But you were joking in that piece, weren't you?"

Caught. Of course he was but now that Sam said it, he

couldn't confess. "No. I was speculating, that's all. A what-if kind of thing. But I didn't suspect all these other people would find C2C as interesting as I do."

"Interesting? The guy sounds like some mumbling stoner. Is that interesting to you?"

"Dad, unfair. He has some very sharp and cogent perceptions," Amanda said, trying to wedge her way back into the conversation.

"Like the last one?" Sam said. "What, retire the word hero? That's sharp? That's an insult to the brave men and women who have sacrificed their lives for you and me and our freedoms."

"He didn't mean anything like that, Sam," Gary said. "He meant that we do our service men and woman a disservice when we put them on this pedestal and don't consider them human beings."

"Okay, look," Sam said, the knife handle still drumming his consternation. "This is all going to be settled in court and I'm sure C2C will be a thing of the past by next week at this time. But in case it isn't I want to make sure you two know what you're doing. It may all be a lark to you right now, but if this keeps up you could be more destructive to the country than the goddam Republicans and their do-nothing style of governance."

"That's a pretty high bar," Gary said, still not able to leave frivolity behind.

"What?" Sam said, the knife held hovering above the table.

"You'd have to work very hard to screw up the system as well as the Republicans did."

"Well you don't look like you're breaking a sweat. What's it been, nine weeks, something like that, and you've put the country in a tailspin?"

"I haven't done anything, Sam. I wrote a speculative piece. Forces beyond my control have taken over and..."

"Fucked up a perfectly good campaign. Todd Townsend is a good man, a loyal and valuable asset this country desperately needs right now. And what does he have to do? What does his party have to do? Get bogged down in this horseshit, battling some opponent who doesn't exist, who's afraid to show himself?"

"He showed himself, Dad. He wrote about heroes. You didn't agree with him but you weren't complaining about how he dressed, who he loved, what his background was. You had a problem with his idea. Which is the way it should be. Why do you need to see him?"

"Amanda, you were a great student and you're a certified genius, but on this matter you're a dunderhead. How the fuck is C2 fucking C ever going to govern? What are we going to see when we turn on the nightly news, a laptop on a desk in the oval office? Hal? What do we call him, or her, President Blog?"

"Dad, who turns on the nightly news?"

"Well, I do. And I hope you do. And I know my constituents do."

"But C2C's supporters don't. The stuff on the nightly news is last hour's news. It's just filler for Viagra commercials."

"That's not true. We aren't there yet. And we aren't at the point where the president of the United States is anonymous. Please tell me you agree with that. Please say that this guy or girl or robot or whatever the fuck it is will reveal himself or be revealed before we get to that point. Look me in the eye, you two. You know the guy. Tell me. Is this C2C anywhere near presidential timber?"

Amanda couldn't hold her father's gaze and looked over at Gary. Gary had no problem locking stares with the congressman.

"Yes," Gary said. "He, or she, is."

The reaction to C2C's win in New Hampshire was swift and hyperbolic. Todd Townsend's campaign, backed by what the *Times* called "deep pocket players," blanketed the country with lawyers, all of them running around trying to find out who to sue, where to protest, how to attack. The Democratic National Committee found itself in the uncomfortable position of being asked to disqualify a candidate who clearly had the support of a large swath of the party's membership and thus risk losing those voters. Jill Castle, who got 11 percent of the New Hampshire vote, said that she had really come in second to Townsend, who ended up with 28 percent of the vote and so she was going to stay the course. Don Michaels, in one of the larger gaffes of the campaign so far, quit the race saying that the country had failed him, that "little people" should have more respect for "those of us who have demonstrated our ability to win big in the markets."

The Republicans, who were in the midst of nominating Chuck Haynes, a Senator from South Carolina who defiantly wore a Confederate flag belt buckle everywhere he went, were glad to see someone beside themselves labeled dysfunctional. An upstart group in the GOP was calling for Republican voters in South Carolina to write-in C2C just to poke a finger in the establishment's eye. The airwaves were filled with so many pundits, experts, academicians, pollsters, and forecasters that it seemed at times like the entire population of Washington was on the air or on the page somewhere in the world at the same time.

The world itself was delighting in the spectacle of the self-proclaimed "greatest democracy in the history of man" getting tripped up by people calling for that democracy to change and grow. That is, the people of the world were enjoying the show. The leaders of many countries, however, were aghast at the swiftness with which the transformation in America was happening. Arab Spring had been one thing as far as social media activism was concerned. They had been able to quash a lot of that rebellion or at least submarine it after a brief, superficial revolution. But C2C's powerful showing and impact on the state of the nation was a different matter. These worldwide leaders who were adept at marginalizing and maiming their opposition felt for the likes of Todd Townsend whose battle cry had become "where is C2C?" You can't marginalize and maim if you don't know where the goddam opposition is.

Gary's brief appearance outside the Concord Radisson had quickly become a touchstone for the movement. The country singer Bart Hanson posted a video of Gary telling the crowd that

"C2C thanks you" with a ditty Hanson had penned called, "No C2C, we thank you!" Gary did a couple of the big talk shows, the late nights and the Sunday mornings, thinking that would satisfy the hungry media, but they only prompted requests for more interviews. Finally, twelve days before the South Carolina primary, he published an op-ed in the Washington Post reiterating his reasons for supporting C2C and declaring he would have nothing more to say until after South Carolina.

While the interviewers had all been ostensibly talking to Gary about the philosophy behind the phenomenon, about what he believed, about what he saw in store for a post-paper, post-money political world, what all of them really wanted to know was who C2C was. The search for whoever was behind the blog intensified tenfold after New Hampshire. No one could believe that a world full of hackers couldn't locate the author of a simple blog. And no one could believe that the author could keep such a low profile that no one close to him or her hadn't realized who was in their midst. The sheer fact that such a thorough and deep search had turned up nothing led to all sorts of nut job theories about alien invasions, AI takeovers, and shadowy underground webs in control of the internet.

Gary, meanwhile, had slowly come to realize what his little outburst in Concord meant; that he was on the hook for C2C's identity. His days were plagued by imagined scenarios of various stripes, none of which was all that appealing. Option one was that C2C was never found, never raised his hand, and Gary stayed mum to, supposedly, respect C2C's wishes. That would provide no resolution for either Gary or the country and he prayed that one didn't come true. He could see himself forty years hence, a drunk at the end of the bar, still waiting for his own personal Godot to arrive. Option two was even scarier. The real C2C is found and he or she is some clueless crank, some idiot you wouldn't want driving you to work much less running the country. In that case Gary would be a punchline for the rest of his life. Option three seemed at first to be the best, that C2C turns out to be a good guy, able to fulfill the office. But then it becomes the worst when it becomes clear he or she is somebody who proves to be business as usual, a politician at heart who reverses all the gains of the first few months of the campaign and loses the election to Chuck Haynes.

Gary had become a believer in his own philosophy. Amanda was still of the opinion that the permanent government would not let something as radical as a C2C candidacy and presidency take place, but Gary was seeing a different future. The more his opponents howled about his joke, his stunt, his irresponsible provocation, the more he began to see what he was doing as vital to the progress of the nation. Serious political thinkers were beginning to line up with him and say what a portent the campaign might be. Where some saw a scary future world of cyber government and bot representation, Gary saw a day in which information widened and deepened the political landscape, and the realm of ideas and idea-driven policy triumphed.

Amanda found it increasingly difficult to argue with Gary about these matters and accused him of drinking his own Kool-aid. She insisted they watch both "All The Kings Men" and "All The President's Men" for the umpteenth time, but that didn't seem to have any effect. Gary hadn't spun out of control by any means, but he was defending a position more than he was doing any real thinking about the problems C2C's ascendency raised. After the dinner with her father, Amanda told Gary he'd gone way too far saying that he knew who C2C was and Gary admitted he may have made a mistake. But he defended himself by saying he was certain that C2C would either be found or reveal himself after the South Carolina primary.

"If he wins, the thing is just going to be too big for him to keep on hiding. And if he loses it doesn't make any difference."

Amanda threw up her hands and went to bed. Gary flitted around from online news outlets to broadcast and cable TV shows, gulping down big drafts of the C2C phenomenon. He was still up at 3:00 when Ginny Evans called.

"Did I wake you?" she opened. "I forgot the time difference."

"Actually I was awake. What's up?"

"I'm going to be flying to Boston tomorrow. I can't believe a woman of science like myself is doing this, but I've got to do it."

"Good, but why the trip?"

"A hunch. Can you believe it? A hunch."

"Lots of breakthroughs have come from hunches. Are you telling me your hunch has something to do with C2C?"

"I am and my embarrassment is great."

"Ginny, we go way back. There's no embarrassment with me. Are you going to tell me more?"

"No. You wouldn't understand most of it anyway. But I'll say this. That last C2C post was different from all the others in a very, very subtle way. I don't know if anyone else picked up on it the way we did, but if so I don't think they'll reach the same conclusion we did. Got that?"

"Not really. Who's we?"

"My assistants and I. I'm a full professor. I get perks, like whip-smart grad students who will spend sleepless nights reading through miles and miles of code for pizza money. If I get the Nobel for this I'm going to have to include them in the award."

"The Nobel?"

"A joke, Gar. Everybody out here thinks everything they're doing will get them a Nobel. I don't think running down C2C will make the folks in Stockholm take notice. But it's very cool science. Let me tell you one thing I know for sure. C2C is someone with a very sophisticated grasp of computer science. Or knows someone who knows a shitload. That's why I'm going to Boston."

"Huh?"

"Yeah, that didn't follow, did it? Anyway, all our digging has led me to a hunch and I'm going to follow it."

"And the hunch is?"

"I did graduate work at M.I.T. as you know. And I did a cooperative project with a grad student at Tufts. This was ten years ago, in the Pleistocene era of computers. We set up a part of the

Tufts infrastructure, computer infrastructure, for our own needs and I thought by now it would have been trashed long ago. But we might just have found a vestige of it in that last post from C2C. Or not. But I'm going to go have a look."

"You've got to go there?"

"No, of course not. But it'll make the book a lot better if I do."

"The book?"

"I've got a contingent contract, Gar. With one of the big six for a pile if I nab C2C."

"Oh."

"I'll let you know when I get to Boston. How are things with you? Seems like I don't have to ask that. I can't get away from you in the news. And by the way you rocked on Colbert."

"Yeah. What are the chances you'll know whether your hunch is right by the 21st?"

"You mean before South Carolina?"

"Exactly."

"I don't have a clue. Well, I have a clue, but I don't have a timeline. I...just sit tight. Also, I can't believe I'm the only one seeing this in the data, so prep yourself for somebody else beating me to your man."

Gary didn't sleep much the rest of the night. He knew Ginny was a very cautious woman who wouldn't have picked up the phone without something more than a hunch. On the other hand she was now chasing a book deal as well as C2C and maybe her normal caution was being warped by the lure of fame and dollar signs. It has happened before.

As the sun rose Gary trolled through his set of sites to see what sort of buzz C2C had created overnight. One of those sites was called Terra Firma. It was a blog by one of the most feared political pit bulls in Washington, Terry Rogers. Gary thought most of her digging, comments and exposes were reprehensible but he had it on his list mainly for sentimental reasons. As a "g and t" student, gifted and talented, his parents had sent him to a camp full of teenage nerds and Terry was the only camper he connected with. Connect in this case was literal. Terry had given him his first blowjob on a sweet, innocent afternoon in sun-dappled woods. They had not had much to do with each other since, but every time they did cross paths Terry would subtly make Gary aware that she had that blow job in her back pocket and could use it any time she wanted. In the post he was reading, as Amanda woke and started coffee, Terry hadn't pulled out the blow job card, but she didn't have to. She had a lot of other ammunition.

This Has Got To Stop

As I wrote in my last post, Terra Firma is very close to determining the identity of C2C, or as we like to call It here CULater. If you're at all interested in the coward who won't run for office but has been wildly successful at pulling strings behind a curtain of anonymity, then stay tuned and you'll soon have your curiosity rewarded. Don't bother with the likes of Gary King, who is nothing but one of the puppets CULater has been parading around the country as his surrogate. Those factotums won't get you straight answers and surely won't allow you to see the larger picture.

The larger picture. People voting for CULater will tell you (and clueless reporters will dutifully write what these people say ad nauseam) that they are part of a revolution in American politics, that the "old ways" of electing our president, and by implication all elected officials, is outdated, kaput, held captive by monied interests, and that by voting for a non-candidate they are sending a message to the "elite" that this age-old method has to stop. If you hear that claptrap, change the channel.

What has to stop is our silly fascination with the rule breakers and their enablers. From a distance, say that of China or Europe, the Iowa and New Hampshire primaries in the Democratic party look like recognizably childish behavior, a sort of temper tantrum by those who either didn't prevail in their aspirations or those who, like the worst actors in the '60's, simply want to tear down institutions in order to tear down institutions. What is so unnerving in our current dilemma is that the "kids" trying to destabilize, demoralize and destroy American democracy are in large measure fully grown adults, people who should know a true champion of freedom from a mountebank. Fueled by nothing more than a watery blog and a misused social network, they have thrown a monkey wrench, sand, and glue into the gears of the most reliable electoral process the world has ever known.

This has got to stop. Those of us who thought the judiciary would provide balance to the situation were, of course, disheartened by the ruling in federal district court in Atlanta this week affirming the right of voters to write-in the candidates of their choice. In the over 250 years of the Republic no one has taken the write-in vote right as anything more than a form of free speech; you can ignore the stated candidates and enter one of your choosing, but you are simply making a statement, not expecting a result.

And even if you were expecting a result it would be because you knew the non-candidate you were writing in, knew his or her strengths, background, foibles, and abilities. But the most pernicious nature of CULater is Its dark anonymity. Oh, yes, the likes of Gary King say we are privy to some of Its most intimate and searching "Ideas" but we have no guarantee of their authenticity, of the character of their creator. The Kings of the country (isn't it appropriate that the non-leader of the C2C movement, the man who wouldn't be king, has a royal surname) would have us believe that there is a purity in what they are doing, that they are giving the country an IV bag full of truth straight to the vein. Bullshit.

The people who have wasted their vote so far are going to wake up soon, as the muddied, Monday morning crowd at Woodstock did, and see that their voice is gone and the ecstatic moment was a hollow thump. They will, I guarantee you, want that vote back when they see the damage done. That damage is hard to calculate fully at this point. At some point the parties and the judiciary will have to put a halt to this mass stupidity, but where will the good people who should be getting all the attention, the real candidates, be then?

Vice President Townsend has been saying recently that he can't keep asking donors to plow their hard earned dollars into his campaign if the primaries ahead are going to be as non-sensical as the first two. "I'm competing against a ghost," he told a South Carolina audience Wednesday. This from the Democratic candidate who, if you throw out the votes cast for CULater, won the New Hampshire primary.

Or Senator Jill Castle who came in second in New Hampshire, again, absent CULater, but who is doing almost no campaigning in the remaining primary states because her PAC reported an almost immediate cessation of donor commitments in the aftermath of CULater's stunning "victory" in the Granite State.

Terra Firma is, as you well know, strictly bipartisan, but let me say that these two fine candidates, as well as the three remaining Republican candidates, are excellent specimens of democratic politicians, legislators, and leaders. That they are being swamped at the ballot box, in the media, and in street corner conversations by a candidate who exists, if at all, in zeros and ones, who has, as far as we know never held office, who has never publicly expressed a wish to either be elected or govern, who has given no indication how It would govern if elected, and who, as far as can be learned, has not spent a penny of his or anyone else's money on a campaign, is a tragedy of the first proportion.

Part of this tragedy is that the federal government has not as of yet jumped in to quash the crap. That has left the candidates, with their often shaky coffers, to make the expensive arguments to various courts, to defend not only themselves but the democracy itself. And who loses in that shift of funds? Why the voters, of course, the working stiffs, the same populace being hoodwinked into giving up their precious vote for a handful of air.

As many of you know Gary King and I have been friends since our adolescence. I have watched him progress in his career and have been impressed by one thing in particular; his luck. He supported Fran Wallinger when he was still at Georgetown and before he even graduated became her chief of staff. He left her employ only months before Tinglegate blew up and Wallinger was indicted. Gary skedaddled just in time and was never a target of the Tinglegate investigation. He landed on his feet as an aide to Senator Jim Hawkins just before Hawkins assumed the chairmanship of the Foreign Relations Committee and Gary, most sources agree, was whispering in the Senator's ear throughout the disastrous Pakistan corruption hearings, though none of the brickbats Hawkins suffered landed on his trusted aide.

And then Gary abandoned politics, or so he said, and moved in with his girlfriend, who had conveniently just won a McArthur Genius award for her work with Louisiana feminists and was a half a mil dollars *richer. That sweet domestic situation allowed him time to plot his revenge against the political world he spent such a brief and discordant time in. And the result is C2C.*

Common 2 Cents is a successor to Thomas Paine's Common Sense in one sense only. The author of the blog is, as was Paine, anonymous. Paine had very good reason to hide his identity. His ideas were not only revolutionary but seditious and he risked his life to publish his pamphlet. C2C, on the other hand, is in more danger being anonymous than he would be unmasked. When we know the scalawag behind the blog we'll see him or her for the mushy thinker It is. It has taken full advantage of the internet's propensity for identity obfuscation and more, going so far as to digitally encrypt Its blog so tightly one wag has suggested it's the result not of writing but of a computer loop gone rogue. But Its only real fascination is its anonymity.

All this has to stop. The country needs leadership not headless horsemen. I am certain that I will have CULater's identity soon, that judges will put a stop to the inanity, and that we will have normally–nominated candidates in some seven months. But I'm not sure what the effect of all this will be and for that uncertainty I blame my old camp mate Gary King. It was he who set flame to a tinder of his own making, he who fanned the fire by his own mysterious disappearance in the run-up to the primaries, and he who will have to answer for the long-term damage to the electoral process.

So, as I said. Stay tuned, folks. You know my sources are deadly accurate and sturdily reliable. And they are dedicated to their current task because they, as much as anyone in the country, know this madness has got to stop.

Gary didn't believe Terry was close to identifying C2C but you couldn't say for sure. She had pried a lot of ultra secret information from the tightly held fists of very powerful people. She had persuaded camera-shy wrongdoers to answer her questions. From Gary's perspective C2C's identity looked like a cake-walk for her. But the fact that she hadn't yet revealed the name, that she had only said she was on the trail, made him think she was not close to a coup. Plus, symbolically enough, Terry was most adept at plying her trade within the Beltway and outside the cyber world. What did she know about computers? What did she know about the world beyond the Potomac? She seemed to give a nod to this indirectly by attacking him. She wasn't going to be a big problem.

Amanda had been talking on the phone briefly while making coffee and came to the kitchen door with her phone in her hand, reading something. She stopped, finished reading and looked up.

"Well," she said. "It could have been worse. She could have mentioned your small dick."

4

It was cold and rainy as Ginny Evans drove out to Medford to begin her search at Tufts. She felt badly about lying to Gary on their phone call the night before. She hadn't come all the way across the country on a hunch. She was riding some very solid evidence and she was making a personal appearance because that evidence turned up a character Ginny wanted to get to know better.

Ginny hadn't lied to Gary about the route her search had taken. She had in fact found a fingerprint of sorts in the encrypted blog posts, one she recognized from her graduate school days. She hadn't been worried about encryption but her partner on the project back then had been a certified paranoid who was certain someone would hack their work and dash his hopes for his Ph.D. Now Ginny was glad the guy had been so anxious because the Gerry-rigged encryption they had set up was as identifiable a Coke bottle in a wine cellar, if you knew what you were looking for.

And the person who was now wielding that encryption system was savvy enough to use it instead of the whistles and bells numbers everybody else used these days. No wonder the world had reached a dead end in its search for C2C. The blog was actually sort of limping along the side of the road, encryption-wise, when everybody was looking for some Mazerati zipping down the highway. Once Ginny realized this she marveled at two things; first the coincidences that brought her to the search, her brief fling with Gary years back, his phone call, her interest and then her having been in contact with the Tufts system in graduate school, and secondly the way in which the encryption mirrored the folksy, common sense milieu of the blog itself.

While reading the blog had at first convinced Ginny that its author was a man, after finding the fingerprint and trying to imagine who had used it, she became certain that the author was a woman. As she circled several blocks looking for parking near the Tufts campus she felt that in one respect she hadn't lied to Gary. She hadn't had the hunch she had told him about, but she had had a hunch that the woman behind the blog might be someone for her, a woman with a mind like her own, a possible partner. Such romanticism had become a part of Ginny's life ever since she realized who she was and what she was looking for in a partner. Now here she was, probably very close to the epicenter of the frenzied phenomenon known as C2C and her mind was wandering to shared lives and domestic bliss. If the powers that be at CalTech ever found out about this it might be grounds for having her tenure revoked.

The crude computer lab she and the other graduate student had worked in was no longer where it had been. She got directions to the new one and had to walk through a spitting rain all the way across the campus to a place called Halligan Hall. It took her a while to sweet talk her way into the main lab and a little longer to find a sympathetic lab assistant who would allow her to use one of the stations. She had dropped her name and CalTech and the assistant, who was aware of her papers, was impressed.

"Why would you come all this way when you've got that fantastic lab out there?" he asked, a naïve question that assumed she was just jetting around the country looking for another lab to plop down in.

"Sentimental reasons," Ginny answered, which was sort of true.

It took her a couple of hours to map the system and to figure out which work station was the most likely source for C2C. No one was using it at the time and Ginny tried, unsuccessfully, to crack its user logs, but that information was pretty tightly held. She decided to go low tech and stake out the work station to see who showed up to use it. The station sat in a corner cubicle, sort of off by itself, and as Ginny read and caught up with work emails on a nearby station she thought of the C2C station as the quiet, patient partner of the woman who was turning the American political scene upside down.

After about an hour a man sat down at the work station and stared at the screen for a long time without typing. Ginny couldn't see what he was looking at. When he left twenty minutes later she slid into his still-warm seat, pulled up the recent history and expected to get some porn site. What she found instead was a long, very technical article in French on a leading computer science site in Europe. She decided the man was most definitely not a candidate for C2C.

Around five in the afternoon, with her eyelids drooping from jet-lag and her stomach growling from hunger, she decided her day of old school sleuthing was over. She realized that anyone wanting to keep his or her identity secret would probably work deep in the night, that she was leaving way too early, but her body was telling her to find a hotel. As she reached the front of the building she peered out through the glass front doors to see how much rain was falling, how wet she was going to get reaching her car. She started to go through a turnstile just as a man in his thirties and his six or seven year-old son started through from the other side. The little boy darted under the prongs.

"Hey, Max, come on," the man said. "Be polite." And then to Ginny. "Sorry."

The boy piped up behind them. "Come on, Dad. We gotta get the right one."

The man smiled at his son and started through the turnstile just as Ginny did the same. The two did a little after-you-Alphonse dance before Ginny went through. Then she stopped, turned and watched the two of them go down the hall, the boy excited.

Ginny hesitated, something telling her she should follow the father and son, see where they were going. Then she told herself that if this man was indeed C2C the coincidences would be simply too mind-boggling. She turned and walked out the second front door. But she hadn't gotten far before she remembered what the boy had said. "We gotta get the right one." She remembered a C2C post about fatherhood. She was torn, go back or not. Then she told herself that she was three thousand miles away from home because of some intuition and there was no reason why she shouldn't go a few more feet if that same intuition told her to do so. She went back in the building, once again got the security guard to let her in, and went down the hallway to the lab. As she walked she told herself that if the dad and son weren't at the corner work station, she'd just turn around and leave.

But there they were, the boy on his dad's lap. Ginny's skin prickled. She sat a ways away. She waited long minutes, watching. Both father and son seemed to be glued to the screen, their concentration extraordinary. Ginny couldn't help but feel she was doing something millions of people around the country would have given their eye teeth to do, discovering C2C's identity.

"Ginny?"

The voice came to her as if from another world. She had been so concentrated on the scene in the cubicle she forgot she was in a public space. She turned to see a bearded man, looking down at her.

"Yes," she answered.

"They said you were here and I couldn't believe it. Rob Edelman."

Ginny had to take a couple of seconds to put the name with the face, thinking first it was someone whom she had met at a conference. Then she realized Rob was the graduate student she had worked with.

"Rob, geez, yeah. Sorry. The beard."

"I know. Fools a lot of people. I need it to look older. I'm teaching here now."

He was excited. He asked what Ginny was doing there and she came up with a plausible reason that Rob didn't really swallow. She could see his skepticism and so said she was on a confidential mission. He invited her for coffee. She declined. He wanted to talk, she wanted to keep her eye on the cubicle, and so they stood there for fifteen minutes or so, gabbing about the old days, until Rob looked at his watch, mumbled something about being an absent-minded professor and how he had to pick up his kid from basketball practice and took off.

Ginny watched until he was out of the lab, then turned back. The cubicle, of course, was empty and Ginny started dashing around trying to find the father and son but to no avail. Finally she went back to the work station, went to the station's history and found that whatever the two had been working on was gone.

Ginny's head ached and she felt the precursor chills of a cold. But she was warmed by one very unscientific fact; she was sure she had been in the presence of C2C.

5

The email came into an account Gary and Amanda had set up only days earlier, one they had intended only for their communication with each other, one they felt was as secure as it could possibly be.

To: Gary

From: C2C

Mr. King,

I am a Republican and I am not interested in running for office. Please stop your efforts immediately. Thank you.

At first Gary thought Amanda was punking him and he got a kick out of the humor. Then he didn't recognize the email account it had come from. Then he called Amanda, who was in Louisiana for work, and when she said she had nothing to do with the email, was in a meeting and would call back in the evening, Gary stared at the screen on his laptop and wondered if the thing could be legit. And if it was, what did that mean?

He forwarded the email to Ginny and asked if she could locate the sender and if it looked like the real deal. Ginny called a half-hour later and sounded like her nose was plugged with gauze, her throat lined with sandpaper.

"The account this came from was shut down fifteen minutes after the email to you was sent," she said.

"By who?"

"The user."

"Which means you can't trace it," Gary asked.

"Probably not," Ginny said. "I can hardly get out of bed up here. I came down with a doozy last night."

"How's it going otherwise?"

"Sympathetic of you."

"Sorry, but this is something I never expected. How could the author of those posts be a Republican?"

"I think a better question is how did this C2C hack your account? You set it up very well, it seems. You're sure nobody but you and Amanda know the password?"

"Yup."

"Did you ever write the password down and leave it some place?"

"I didn't. I don't know about Amanda."

"Well, I don't know. I can't say one way or another. But it sounds like a prank to me."

"Is there any way you can verify it or, I don't know, cross check it with the C2C blog, something like that?"

"There is, but I'm not going to be doing that right away. I came down with a cold up here. A real doozy. Did I tell you that?"

Gary apologized and got off the phone. Ever since he had written the Poli-Ticks article his inbox had been stuffed with harangues of all sorts, as well as good wishes and offers of support, and his spam filter was exhausted from working overtime. But that account had been out there for years and it was easy for practically anyone to get his address and let him have it. This was different and the content of the email was disturbing. He was scheduled to go to South Carolina in two days but he didn't want to go down there if there was a chance that C2C was going to come out of the woods wearing an American flag, toting an AK-47, carrying a picture of a dead fetus, and looking for "the sumabitch put my name on the Democratic ballot." He set up a conference call with his inner circle and got a mixed response. Ed Popper said it had to be a hoax. Wanda Samuels, more savvy about Washington than Ed, thought it had all the feel of a dirty trick, perpetrated by the Republicans. Mark Parish sounded gleeful, his dream of a ring-side seat at a colossal meltdown coming into view. Bella and Vince Cardoza were adamant that C2C was no Republican. All thought Gary should go to South Carolina. Wanda was already there and said the atmosphere was "electric."

"Gary, you've got to see this on the ground," she continued. "Sometimes it's like an alternate universe. People are meeting almost spontaneously. I was in a coffee shop yesterday and you could hear 'C2C' buzzing through every conversation. Then people started leaving their tables, going to other tables, introducing themselves, and talking more about the primary. It looked like that part of a church service where everybody goes around shaking everybody's hands and saying 'Peace' or 'Shalom' or whatever. It was something."

When he talked to Amanda that evening she said it had to be a hoax and that he should go, that she was certainly going herself. She said even in Louisiana C2C was on everybody's lips. "I had a hard time doing the work I wanted to do. Everybody at the conference wanted to talk to me about C2C. Has Ginny turned up anything?"

"No. She's got a cold."

"How's a cold going to stop her?"

"I don't know. I don't know what she's doing up in Boston in the first place. Okay. So, I'm going to ignore this email and go down to South Carolina."

"Good plan. We've got a nice hotel down there. We'll have fun. There'll be a lot more pranks if C2C wins. You're right, just ignore the nonsense."

Easier said than done. After a restless night of little sleep news came mid-morning that Chuck Haynes had called a news conference for noon and promised a startling revelation. Gary caught it live on CNN. The leading Republican candidate, who had in the past month seemed ready to eat C2C for breakfast if he could find him, even though the blogger's presence was going to help his own chances for the Oval Office, was in a cheery, bouncy mood as he stepped to the cluster of microphones and grinned out his news.

"Well, ladies and gentlemen, the jig is up. The author of the blog Common 2 Cents has come forward and would like me to make two things clear to y'all this morning here in the Capital of Southern Hospitality. First he, and the author is a male, would like it to be known that he is a registered Republican and plans to remain so until his dying day. Secondly, he would like any and all of those seeking to draft him for the Democratic ticket to cease and desist, to stand down, to write in his name no more."

Haynes seemed to have really caught the press flat-footed and it took them a long few seconds to absorb the news. They then began firing questions at him about the authenticity of the statement, how Haynes got hold of it, and, of course, the identity of the blogger. Haynes parried all these questions with a folksy, "We'll get y'all the details later. I can understand how you might have your doubts, but trust me, the Dems put this guy out front and, first, he ain't going out front, and secondly he's not gonna be happy with those who voted for him."

Gary couldn't help but see what a brilliant strategy this was. Haynes was a wacko to rival the president from Waco, but he had significant clout and was seen in his party as a man of integrity and solid Christian beliefs. No one believed he would say he'd been in touch with C2C if he hadn't been. So he was going to be taken seriously by a lot of Democrats as well as Republicans. And that was going to throw the South Carolina primary into an even more tizzied state than it already was in. It was a tactic straight out of the Book of Joseph McCarthy, down to the promise-to-reveal-details-later ploy.

After he had spent a minute or two admiring Haynes' political skills, Gary realized that, absent C2C's identity, the media were going to need something to report, something to counter Haynes' assertion and that he, Gary, was that something. It didn't take long for the assault on his phone and email, Facebook and Twitter accounts to begin. He sought Amanda's counsel but she wasn't answering any of his entreaties. Gary's brain trust checked in but none of them had much to offer. Wanda Samuels said the majority of people she talked to in Columbia thought Haynes was a lying sonofabitch on a good day and they didn't believe a word he said. But as the afternoon wore on it was clear the rest of the country didn't know Haynes the way his constituents knew him. The mainstream media was treating the announcement as if it were some divine revelation. Gary realized quickly that his own rather half-hearted, indirect suggestion that he knew C2C's identity was going up against the cocked fist of a political brawler. He needed to get on some sort of solid footing before he got knocked on his ass.

Dinner time came without inspiration or new facts arriving. Gary did a healthy vape hit and decided to brave a light snow and head to the Hog and Heifer, a pub he could shelter in, one in which everybody might know his name but were too busy slamming the Redskins' horrible season just passed to care about something like politics. He was safe. At least he thought he was. Coming in from the cold he saw the usual lineup at the bar, nodded to a couple of familiar faces and sat at an empty seat. A martini on the bar and a woman's coat slung over the stool were his next seat neighbors. He ordered a Stella and hoped the woman would sip her vodka without needing to engage in conversation. The pot was going well with the surroundings and he didn't need any buzzkill.

He was looking up at a Georgetown-Syracuse basketball game on the TV over the bar and didn't realize the woman had returned to her seat. Out of the corner of his eye he saw the martini lift off the bar and then return, but he didn't swivel toward her. He was glad they didn't have the evening news on. He was pretty sure he'd be mentioned in some way, maybe even shown in stock footage, and he'd be caught. The game was a close one and he remembered his days at Georgetown, begging for tickets, screaming his lungs out at games.

He ordered a second beer and as he was waiting for it he turned to the woman next to him.

"I wondered when you were going to take your eyes off the game," she said. She was dressed in a champagne colored silk blouse and a short skirt. A shadow from the bar's uneven lighting fell across her face. Her voice was low, a cashmere purr. Gary was wondering if he should introduce himself as Philip Marlowe when he identified the voice, the dress, the face, the martini. It was Terry Rogers, she of the Terra Firma blog, she of the camp blowjob.

"Terry?"

"Well, at least you've identified me. Would you like me to move to another seat? I'm sure you've got a lot on your mind."

"I do, but stay for one question, huh?"

"I'm not used to answering questions, but shoot." Terry took another sip of her drink, allowing the unbuttoned top of her blouse to separate and reveal a lacy black bra. She held the pose as if Gary were a photographer.

"What are you doing here?"

"Having a drink, same as you."

"I've never seen you in here before. You don't live around here, do you?"

"Is that a requirement?"

"No, but I have the feeling this isn't a coincidence and I have the feeling you're not here to apologize for slandering me and my friend Amanda, so I'm wondering what you want."

"Just to say hello, and to catch up."

"Catch up? Don't you think you should have done that before you wrote your column?"

"May I apologize for that?"

"Sure, but I'd appreciate it if you apologize in print."

"I'll see about that. I won't take back what I said about your shenanigans with C2C, though."

The pot and the beer had mellowed Gary considerably. A crackling little fire in the fireplace added to the glow. Terry was certainly nice to look at, especially since she didn't seem to be wearing her usual compliment of fangs. So she had stalked him. The rest of the world seemed to be doing the same thing. Better to have a drink or two with her than Charlie Rose.

"Any news of interest today?" Gary said. "Could that be why you just happen to be here?"

"Don't flatter yourself. I don't need your reaction to Haynes. He's a nut job and he's just winging it on this one. He probably got the same email you got, only he believed it."

She was good. How she got information about his new account he didn't know, but he did have to give kudos to a reporter who was as far ahead of the game as she appeared to be.

"I take it your sources have informed you that Haynes is off the mark and that by now you know the real C2C."

"Let's drop the bullshit, Gary, okay. You said you knew his identity up in New Hampshire. I said I was close last week. You don't know his identity and neither do I and neither does Mr. Confederate Flag Beltbuckle. That blogger's still just Common 2 Fucking Sense."

Gary could see her martini was down to the twist and had loosened her up a bit.

"Maybe it will turn out to be Thomas Paine himself, come back to give the Union a refresher course."

"I'm no great fan of Paine's," Terry said as she indicated to the bartender she wanted a second. "You lockstep liberals fawn all over the guy but he was dangerous. He cloaked his anarchist tendencies in some cockamamie scheme for government and gave radicals the cover they needed."

"Whoa," Gary said, giving Terry a longer look than was required. She was quite stunning in the firelight, her high cheekbones polished by the glow. Gary was having trouble squaring this image of beauty with the nonsense she had just spouted. "You think we'd be better off if he'd never published Common Sense?"

"Maybe. That shock you? That I'm not glued to some American Revolution orthodoxy?"

"No, but, would you prefer we still be under British rule?"

"In a way, yes. There are many parts of the British system that are vastly superior to our own. C2C's candidacy would have been quashed immediately in Britain, for instance."

"You're probably right about that. The permanent government in Britain is even more entrenched than it is here. Paine understood that, that the elites were in control and would always be unless there was a revolt. That's why he published a pamphlet that could be disseminated to the masses. That's why his pamphlet is still the best-selling book ever in the United States. That's why there were public readings of Common Sense all over the colonies. That's why George Washington had the pamphlet read out loud to his troops, most of whom couldn't read themselves. And that's why C2C has gone viral. Two hundred and fifty years ago the billionaire classes controlled the information much as they do now. Paine found a way to use one of the tools of that control, writing, to leap frog that control. That's what C2C is doing today. But you, writing for the elites, can't see that."

"Me? Writing for the elites? Do you know how many of those elites I've brought to their knees?"

"Shuffling the deck chairs on the Titanic."

"What? I'm feared in this town. I'm the equalizer. I'm standing up for the little guy."

"Oh, please. Be real. You're just a tool. They give you the leaks they want to give you. You're a foot soldier for the status quo. Why else are you going after a phenomenon like C2C other than the fact that he's upsetting the apple cart for all your real constituents."

"I don't have constituents. I have readers. Lots of readers. From all strata of society, if you want to know. I give voice to the voiceless."

"Paine gave voice to the voiceless. C2C gives voice to the

voiceless. You give voice to your ego and whoever whispers in your ear."

Gary realized it was his buzz speaking, but he was happy with the way things came out. He had vented and now Terry seemed uncharacteristically plussed. She took a drink. The fire in the fireplace popped. The jukebox was rolling out Chrissie Hynde. Life was good.

"May I be blunt?" Terry asked.

"Can you be anything but?"

"I can," Terry said, dropping any hint of snark. "You of all people should know my public persona is just that, a guise. I have to bluster in order to be heard. C2C can prattle on in his low-key way because he has you and the gods of viral explosion to promote him. But I'm not Terra Firma. I'm firma about very little. In fact the only thing firma about me is my breasts."

Gary's gaze dropped immediately to the v in Terry's silk blouse and then tried to recover by dropping farther, to the bar, to his beer. Terry smiled over at him.

"You haven't forgotten, have you," she said, waiting for Gary to meet her gaze. When he did she continued. "I certainly haven't. I've been very picky in my life, Gar. I bed hop. I admit that. But the beds I hop in have to be great beds, meaning good guys, solid men, men I'll trust with my body, men like you. You were the first and I'm only sorry for one thing in that summer, that we didn't do the full number. Any time, such as tonight, for instance, you'd like to correct that error let me know. NSA all the way, okay? But know that it's there for you if you want."

"Is this your way of getting me to tell you C2C's identity?" Gary said, twirling his glass. Terry put a soft hand on his, stopping the twirling.

"No, Gary. This is a way to square memory with feeling. I can still see your lovely penis pop out of your trunks, I can still taste your warm cum. I've been looking for that sight, for that taste ever since. I know we'd fit well. How many times in life do you know that, experience that? Yeah we have some political differences but so do Carville and Matalin. You could come to my place right now and I'd show you what I mean."

Gary, the Gary of reason and caution, unexpectedly got up, went to the fireplace, tried to rearrange the burning logs, caught fire and was quickly sent up the chimney in smoke. Gary, the daring one, stayed put and grinned.

"And I assume this will be relayed to your loyal readers. You won't have to quote a source this time, will you? No, 'I have it on reliable information,' but first hand reporting. 'Gary King, the prick ruining things for the people who really run the country, turns out to have a prick, blah, blah, blah.'"

"You clearly don't read Terra Firma religiously. I am always circumspect about sex."

"Circumspect? Don't you mean coy, disingenuous, reeking with innuendo, winkingly malicious?"

"You're getting me hot."

"It's the martini. Those are pejoratives. You should..."

Gary felt a pull on the back of his neck and realized Terry had looped an arm over his shoulder and was pulling him toward her. Before he could react his lips locked with Terry's in a soft wet kiss that he couldn't extricate himself from without what would probably be an embarrassing approximation of wrestling. Plus the thing felt good, the warmth in his chest ballooned, his nethers came awake and he decided a few more seconds of this goodness wouldn't hurt anyone.

Then came the blinding light to his right and Terry's quick pull back. Gary opened his eyes to see Terry hauling in the phone she had just selfied them with, furtively tapping on the screen, probably sending the photo off to the safety of the cloud. Then Terry looked up at him and smiled.

"Did you say yes or no to coming back to my place? I can't remember," she said.

"I didn't say."

"I wasn't kidding about you. Let's see if the second go round is as good as the first."

"Uh, we have a little trust issue."

"Trust?"

"That selfie?"

"Oh, that's just between you and me. Check your email. I just sent it to you. I wouldn't think of sending it to anyone else."

Gary didn't give her the satisfaction of checking his email. He eyed her for a long time. What a strange woman, so driven she can't have normal relationships, so lacking in perspective she can't see herself for the warped individual she is. His gaze also included her lovely neck, the line of those firm breasts and the long, articulated bend of her legs. She was the perfect Washington temptress and who was he to pass on her wiles simply in order to maintain his own fortress of integrity?

"Did you say you lived close by?" he asked.

6

Adam Molloy had been holed up in a motel in Buffalo for days. The snow he'd encountered on the trip out had kept up a steady pace and now, from his motel room window, all he could see were mounds of white. This didn't bother him. He kept away from TV, from the computer, and spent a lot of time reading. He had thought that everything he had come to Buffalo for would be over by now, but it wasn't. He enjoyed being sort of off the grid and asked himself if he had planned things that way, if he was indeed escaping.

Every day the motel office had called and said that the woman who cleans the rooms was stranded and asked if he needed anything. He didn't but on the fourth day there was a knock on the door mid-morning and the wife of the owner of the motel, a tiny woman in a sari, stood there with towels and a bucket of cleansers and said she would clean the bathroom for him. Adam started to protest but she breezed past him before he could speak.

"My name is Maggie," she said, in a lilting Indian accent. "If you need anything, you can call for me. My name isn't really Maggie, but it's close to that."

Adam nodded and closed the laptop he had open on the desk. Maggie saw this, stopped, and eyed him.

"You have something to hide?" she asked.

"No," Adam said.

"People who stay for long times in a motel have something to hide usually."

"Well, I don't. I'm here because my daughter is, uh, about to have a baby."

Maggie gave him another questioning look.

"Why aren't you staying at her house?"

"Because she doesn't know I'm out here."

Maggie shook her head, disbelieving, and went into the bathroom. Adam heard her banging around, talking to herself for the next fifteen minutes. When she came out she seemed even more skeptical.

"Why doesn't she know you're here?"

"It's complicated, but I'm a doctor and..."

"Okay," Maggie said, holding up her hand. "That's enough. What would a doctor be doing in a motel like this? You should be at the Hilton. I don't believe a word you say. You are hiding something."

"I'm not," Adam said, surprising himself that he wanted to convince this woman. "This motel is the closest to the hospital. And look, look at what I've written here." He opened the laptop, not expecting her to actually read what was there. But she bent over and squinted and then looked at him.

"Are you a Buddhist?" she asked.

"No."

"But this is Buddhism. 'The body is not the real.' That is Buddhism."

"It's just my thoughts. I have read in Eastern religions but..."

Maggie shook her head again and left the room, mumbling something about the stories people tell.

Adam relayed the conversation to his wife Michelle when they talked later.

"What were you writing that she called you a Buddhist?"

"Oh, just something."

"You've been writing a lot of 'just somethings' recently. Why the mystery?"

"There's no mystery. I'm just jotting, that's all."

"You let that Maggie read it."

"I didn't exactly let her. She sort of insisted on it."

"Can I insist?"

"I'll show it to you sometime. It's not your sort of thing."

"These days you don't let people read what you write and they're going to think you're C2C."

"Two silly?"

"C2C. The blogger."

"Oh. Right."

"You haven't kept up with the news?"

"A little. South Carolina. He might win. Something like that."

"You are sounding like a Buddhist monk now.

"Nope. I'm still a doctor."

Michelle didn't speak for long seconds. "Hannah may know where you are."

"Why do you say that?"

"She called this morning and..."

"When?"

"About ten-thirty. She..."

"I spoke to her around noon. She didn't seem any different."

"I know, but I think she's getting suspicious. She asked for you. I said you were at the office. She said she'd call you there and I told her she'd have better luck with your cell. She..."

"What did she say?"

"She was just a little surprised I guess. The way she hesitated made me think maybe she suspects something."

"Well, when I talked to her I didn't get any of that. We had a pretty straight forward father-daughter, doctor-patient talk."

"Adam, it kind of scares me when you talk like that. You're not her doctor."

"I know, but I can answer some of her questions. I'd do the

same thing if I were home and she was calling. Twelve days late is an eternity for a first time mother."

"I know. But you're out there. She doesn't know you are. What could you possibly do if..."

"If anything went wrong? I'd be right there in five minutes."

"But, again, what could you possibly do?"

"Comfort her. Help her maybe. Help Jeff. Get information." Michelle was silent. "I know you're thinking this is all about Hannah's birth, about what happened, and that I'm trying to redo history or something."

"No, I don't think you're trying to redo history, but I think you're letting history redo you. You haven't been yourself for a while now. Is something else going on or is it just anxiety about Hannah?"

"Something else?"

"Yes. The Adam I used to know wouldn't have left his patients for a trip like this, wouldn't have tolerated a motel for days on end. Is this all about Hannah or is there something you're hiding from me?"

"No. Nothing. But I might admit that I'm changing. You get away from the daily grind and you see things that have been in front of you for a long time that you never really noticed before. That can change you."

"This is your Buddhism?"

"Sort of."

Michelle softened her voice.

"Everything's going to be all right, Adam," she said. "Just because things went horribly wrong once doesn't mean they're going to again. I know it's a misreading of probabilities, but you paid a huge price with one birth. You're not going to have to go through that again."

"I hope you're right."

"Hope is just another word for fear."

"Now who's the Buddhist?"

"That was one of C2C's posts," Michelle said.

They hung up and Adam took a minute to thank his lucky stars he'd met Michelle. He looked down at his laptop on the motel room desk. He liked what he had written. It was truthful, at least to him. Was it something the world needed to hear? Who knew? Maybe it was just something between him and Maggie.

7

Ginny spent three tortuous days in bed in her hotel room alternating between a wish that she'd never left sunny California and a desire, a deep desire, to know the man in the cubicle, the father with his son Ginny supposed was C2C. She lived on room service ginger ale and crackers, repeated to herself constantly that a cold will go away by itself in three to five days, something a school nurse once told her and she'd never forgotten. She got a number for Rob Edelman hoping he might be able to go through the work station logs for what Ginny was now calling Ground C2Cero, but, with her head pounding, chills making it difficult to talk, and Rob's too eager demeanor, she hung up knowing that wasn't the route that was going to work.

When the cold had subsided enough that she could walk outside she made a beeline for Halligan Hall and spent as many hours as she could tolerate sitting within sight of Ground C2Cero. She tried to do her own work, on a grant application that was due in days, but her mind couldn't be harnessed for such a mundane task. Dad, whom she had only glimpsed briefly and whose face she didn't really see well, loomed in her thinking and gained stature and importance with every appearance in Ginny's imagination. He had the nation by the tail but calmly sat his kid on his knee as he yanked the electorate around. Ginny hadn't shared the nation's rapturous love affair with the blog when Gary had called her. She signed on for the thrill of the chase. But now, with the flesh and blood blogger in her sights, the blogs took on a new cast. They became little gems, distillations from what looked like an ordinary life. Ginny saw them as compressed code which, when unpacked, opened worlds of new ideas and fresh insights. All of which, Ginny realized, argued against Gary's original thought. It had been the presence of the flesh and blood C2C that made his posts somehow different, deeper for her.

After two days and then one evening that stretched into the next morning in her vigilant state, Ginny was ready to pack it in. Her cold had fled, her office was asking very pointed questions about when she was going to return, her grant application was a mess when she finally sent it off, and Gary was questioning why she was continuing her completely outdated stakeout when South Carolina was just around the corner and he desperately needed her to find the elusive C2C. She gave herself a day, made a non-refundable plane reservation, and prepared to pull an all-nighter.

Of course other people had been using the work station in the meantime. The computer lab was popular most hours of the day and night. Rob Edelman had come in from time to time and clearly had his eye on Ginny. She didn't want to put him off, tell him he played on the wrong team for her, or remind him that he was married, but she thought he might be useful if C2C ever showed up again. Ginny forced herself to study everyone who sat down at C2Cero but she had become convinced that Dad was her man and it was hard to invest much in anyone else.

She was preparing to hunker down for a long night, working through a large so-so latte from a cafeteria in the building, when a pony-tailed blonde, close to Ginny's age, came into the lab, went to C2Cero and asked the burly grad student who was working there how much longer he would be. There were other open stations and so when Ginny saw Miss Pony Tail ask the question she took notice. She didn't hear the response, but Miss Pony Tail took off her winter jacket as if she were about to sit down. She was wearing scrubs and had a stethoscope around her neck. She was Midwestern pretty with an open, unlined face, smiling blue eyes and a calm composure. Nurse? Doctor? Hard to tell. The burly guy obviously thought she was worth a few sentences of his time and he tried to chat her up. She was polite but clearly not interested. She seemed to be itching to get to the computer.

When she finally did she buried herself in the cubicle and for over a half an hour Ginny saw almost no movement from the woman. She'd seen such concentration often among the people she studied with and those she taught, but that sort of intensity always thrilled her. Jumpy, agitated people were a turn-off. She forgot a lot of what she was up to and just stared at the pieces of Miss Pony Tail she could see from her vantage point.

Then her phone, on the desk in front of her, played a distinctive ring tone, one she didn't recognize at first, one she had set up but had only once heard ring. It was an alert that C2C's blog had another post. She went to the post but before she could read it she saw out of the corner of her eye that Miss Pony Tail was getting up and putting on her coat. Ginny put the two occurrences together and felt certain that Miss Pony Tail had just sent a post to Common 2 Cents. Ginny fumbled for her own coat and swept up the things she had on the desk, scooping them into her purse as she stumbled over a couple of desk chairs and followed the woman out of the lab.

Miss Pony Tail, who looked like she was a runner, was certainly a walker and Ginny had to skip-walk to keep up with her as she headed down the several hallways to the building entrance. The chase continued outside where the darkened evening was crisp. Ginny struggled to get her coat on and keep pace with her prey. The two, about fifty yards apart, crossed a couple of quads, a city street, and then another open area in front of a hospital complex. Miss Pony Tail took the stairs to the building two at a time and Ginny wondered if she knew she was being followed. There was a revolving door at the front entrance and after Miss

Pony Tail whirled through Ginny tried to follow quickly, maybe even say something to her, but her bag nearly got caught and she had to slow to push it through. By the time Ginny got into the lobby of the building, Miss Pony Tail was using a key card to go through a turnstile. Ginny could see elevators straight ahead and knew she wouldn't be able to get through the turnstiles, which were guarded by a no-nonsense looking woman in blue, before Miss Pony Tail went up. Her mouth opened by itself.

"Doctor," she said, loudly, toward Miss Pony Tail, who turned and glanced at Ginny, then continued. Ginny was about to go with the second option and call out "Nurse," but Miss Pony Tail stopped and took a couple of steps toward Ginny.

"You were talking to me?" she asked.

Ginny was struck by the beauty of the woman's face, which, even in the ugly fluorescence of the lobby, had a warmth you could feel from yards away. For a moment Ginny had no idea why she was where she was, what she wanted from this woman, why she was calling to her. Then she came to her senses and, standing behind the turnstile, clutching her bag, still a little winded from the sprint across campus, got some words out.

"Oh. You're, uh. Are you Doctor Simon?" That was Ginny's doctor's name.

"No," the woman said and Ginny could see an id badge on a lanyard poking out from the left lapel of the woman's coat. Miss Pony Tail's photo was visible but only "Dr. Pot..." was readable.

"Not Dr. Simon, huh?" Ginny said, unaccustomed to lying, sounding to herself like some madwoman. "I, uh, was looking for Dr. Simon."

"I gathered. You didn't find her," Dr. Pot... said, but without any sign of annoyance. "There's a directory over there," she continued, pointing to a backlit sign with a slew of names on it. "I don't know a Dr. Simon, though. Sorry."

She turned so quickly and was gone in such few seconds that, after the elevator doors had closed Ginny took a couple of moments to reality check, to convince herself she hadn't been chasing some ghost across the breadth of Tufts University.

But she hadn't and the directory coughed up the name Eve Potter. Ginny took out her phone to make a note and remembered the Common 2 Cents post. She had to read it a couple of times to make sense of it. It was almost like haiku and didn't seem to fit with the posts that had preceded it or the woman who had a stethoscope around her neck and could walk faster than Ginny could run.

But something, another one of those damned hunches, told Ginny she had just exchanged a few words, a very few words, with the real C2C.

8

Gary drove to South Carolina two days before the primary, stopping at the airport in Columbia to meet Amanda's plane coming in from Louisiana. Wanda had set them all up in the Hampton Inn near the airport. The media and the other campaigns were downtown but Gary wanted to be away from that scrum, close enough that they could respond if need be but not apt to run into reporters in the bar.

Amanda's plane was early and she was at the baggage claim when Gary reached her. She held up her phone.

"What do you think?"

Gary didn't get it. He reflexively reached for his own phone, remembered he had turned it off while driving, turned it on and looked at Amanda. "What is it? Another post?"

Amanda nodded as Gary's phone played the ringtone he'd set for any new C2C post. It took him less than a minute to look at the post and then look up at Amanda.

"Think it's real?" she asked.

Gary was already clicking around to his preferred group of authenticators, including Ginny, and the early consensus was that it was definitely legit.

"Yeah," he said, reading the post again. "Wonder what Haynes is going to do with this one. Doesn't sound like a Republican wrote this."

" 'The changeless will save us,' doesn't sound like a Democrat wrote it either."

"I like it. Maybe it's a reminder to us as well as the country that what we're going through is all, in the end, ephemeral and that we really need to keep our eye on the big picture, like, not the general election or anything, but reality."

"No one can accuse him of stumping for votes with this one."

"You didn't kiss me," Amanda said.

Gary looped an arm around her shoulders and kissed her temple. "Your fault for showing me that post. How was the trip?"

"Spectacular. After a while nobody cared if I was involved with C2C and we did some great groundwork. I think we're going to have the program running in about ten parishes before the year's out."

Gary spotted Amanda's bag, went to the carousel, grabbed it and dragged it back to Amanda. "Let me guess," he said. "You bought some books."

She smiled, then dropped the smile when she saw three men in business suits, all in their thirties, coming toward them, eyes on Gary. "Trouble at ten o'clock," she said, and Gary turned as the men, overfed frat brothers it seemed, reached them. The leader, a sandy-haired, blue-eyed charmer with his tie loosened, stuck out his hand.

"You're Gary King, aren't you?" Gary nodded. "I'm Paul Martin, friends call me Pinkie. How're you doing?"

He had a light Southern accent and a salesman's bounce. Gary shook his hand. "Fine. Doing fine. This is..."

"Oh, we know. This is Amanda, the genius. Glad to meet you. The brains behind the operation, right?"

Though they were the same age he was, Gary thought he was listening to a Babbit from the fifties. Amanda shook his hand but Gary could see her revulsion. He started to pick up the suitcase.

"Good to meet you all, fortuitous, I think," Pinkie said, not bothering to introduce his companions. "We're all down here for the same reason, right?"

"I don't know," Gary said. "I don't know why you're down here."

"C2C, of course," Pinkie said. "And like I say, fortuitous. You see his latest, just come in this morning? Course you did. Sorry. You got a line straight to the guy, right?"

"No. We..."

"Oh, come on. Wink, wink. I'm not asking you to share. We'll find out soon enough. We don't have a good head of steam like you all but we're going to do real well come Tuesday."

Gary was aware that C2C was attractive to a wide swath of voters but he was having trouble placing these guys in that swath. What was their angle? They looked like middle managers or hucksters who probably had a minor amount of influence in some state legislature and now thought they were ready for the big stage. Of course he, Gary, could be accused of such irrational aspirations, but these guys seemed completely clueless.

"What are you going to do?" Gary asked finally.

"Just what you're doing. Just what you're doing," Pinkie said, and Gary was reminded that he was in the South where repeating a sentence was taught in grade school.

"How's that?"

"You know, encouraging folks to write C2C in."

"Oh. Good. That's what we're here for, right?"

The three little piggies nodded together and Pinkie beamed. "Well," he said. "It may not be good for you all."

"Why's that?"

"Well, we're with R2C2C. You know us?"

"No."

"Republicans Too for C2C? Get it. It's sort of a play on R2-D2 in Star Wars."

"But, they changed the rules this year. Did you know that? This isn't an open primary any more. You can't vote in the Democratic..."

"Hell no. We don't want to vote in y'all's primary. C2C's not a Democrat neither. We're urging people to write him in the Republican one."

Gary looked at Amanda. She shrugged and shook her head. "You're going to write C2C into the Republican primary?" he asked.

"We and a good chunk of the Republican voters. Ever since we learned he was a Republican we said, whoopee, he's for us."

"But what about Chuck Haynes?" Gary asked.

The three men looked at each other and grinned the grins of the knowing. Pinkie interpreted.

"Haynes is a has been. And he's ruffled a lot of feathers. Especially down here. But nobody wants them other bozos and so they all say their gonna vote for Haynes. And you know as well as I do that whoever wins South Carolina for the Republicans wins the nomination. This state's a kingmaker when it comes to the Republicans. So when C2C came out and said he was a Republican, we said he's the only one can block Haynes in South Carolina. So here we are."

"But what about what C2C says? His posts? His, well, his message?"

"His message? We don't care about his message. Can he beat the sonofabitch? That's the question we asked. And sure enough, he can. It's his brand we're talking about. We've got a grassroots wildfire going on as we speak. Won't show up in the polls probably, but you wait and see."

Gary was more explicit with Amanda this time. "Have you heard anything about this," he asked, knowing she hadn't, stalling for a little while to think about the ramifications of Pinkie's claim.

"No," Amanda said. "But I have a question. Which PAC put you up to this and how much are they paying you?"

"Paying us?" Pinkie asked, as if the exchange of money was the farthest thing from his mind.

"Another candidate? Maybe some fat cat with a grudge? The Koch brothers? Who?"

Pinkie canvassed the other little piggies. "Anybody paying you guys?" They shook their heads no. Pinkie turned back to Amanda. "Nope. We're clean. We just want what's best for the country."

"You believe this news that C2C is a Republican?" Gary asked.

"That's why we're here."

"But it came from Chuck Haynes."

"Ain't that the shits? Pardon my French. Shows Haynes really doesn't know his ass from a tea kettle, doesn't it?"

"What are you going to do if C2C wins both primaries?"

"Well, he can't. He's a Republican."

"But he says he doesn't want to run. I mean if you believe what Chuck Haynes says, that he's a Republican, you gotta believe what he says about running."

"Gotta? No. Haynes probably made that part up so nobody would get the idea to write him in the Republican primary."

Pinkie beamed the self-satisfied smile of a high school debater who's just scored a major point.

"I go back to his message," Gary said. "Why would Republicans want C2C in office?"

"You see his post today, didn't you? The guy's a conservative. He says it plain and clear. Change is for lib'rals and radicals. Whatever doesn't change is where we want to be going. It's about fundamentals, the Constitution, the Bible, democracy, freedom. Those things don't change. No. He's a conservative all right."

Gary stared at Pinkie for a few seconds. This, he realized, was the key to C2C's success. Without trying to be phonily inclusive, C2C had managed to speak to a very wide range of the populace. Or, put another way, C2C was a screen on which anyone could project their own worldview and make his posts relevant to them. Some recent polls in South Carolina and in the nation indicated that C2C was as popular with blacks and Hispanics as he was with Deep South whites and anti-abortion groups. Pinkie and the Pinkettes were clearly projecting their own agendas onto C2C just as many millions around the country were doing. Maybe Gary was among them. Maybe C2C didn't have any message you were supposed to dig out of his or her writing. Maybe he was more the Socratic teacher than a lecturer, drawing out people's thoughts and desires through his or her own musing. Gary, a little later, after they'd shed Pinkie, fumbled through this sort of thinking with Amanda, but she stuck to her follow-the-money take on the Pinkie question.

Gary and Amanda didn't go right to their motel, but drove around a little to see if there was as much evidence of the C2C campaign Wanda claimed was ubiquitous. There certainly was. The variety of lawn signs, hand-made ones, dwarfed the manufactured signs for all the other candidates in number and creativity. One of the best they saw was a large sign in a store window in which the two "C's" had been fashioned into eyes, the "2" was a nose and the resulting caricature looked to be both searching and secretive, probing and anonymous. Somebody was going to get an A on their graphic design project. On the Gervais Street Bridge that spanned the Congeree River, there was a long quote from C2C, broken up into ten sentences, each sentence affixed to one of the lampposts along the bridge so that as you drove west to east you could read the quote the way you used to read Burma Shave ads along the roads in the 50's. Gary had never seen the Burma Shave ads in person but he'd heard about them and he thought the technique was perfect for C2C. The signage was all about an idea, not a personality.

They reached their Hampton Inn as the sun was setting and wispy pink clouds floated above the motel. Gary was in an expansive, optimistic mood.

"I think we're going to win this thing," he said as he and Amanda were hauling luggage into the lobby.

"We're not going to win anything, Gar," Amanda replied. "Remember that? It's not us."

"Yeah, yeah. But I can't help having a little ego boost seeing all those signs. Nine weeks ago..."

"Gary. Don't go there. If you're going to take responsibility for all that's going on, rather than see it as the information age phenomenon it really is, you're also going to have to take responsibility for what happens next, if C2C does win. We're talking about the foundations of our democracy being soundly rattled. Are you ready for that?"

"I'm ready for anything," he said, with a grin that had Amanda frowning.

Ten minutes later he realized he wasn't prepared for everything. They had made it into the suite Wanda had reserved for them and greeted Wanda, Mark Parish, and Ed Popper, who, this time, had brought along another girlfriend, Megan, who "worked in film." Bella and Vince had gotten stuck in Buffalo when their flight was cancelled. Gary had expected the room to be in high spirits but nobody was bouncing off the walls and some of the looks he got were icy. When Wanda pulled him into the bedroom he found out why.

"Have you seen her post?"

"Whose?" Gary asked.

Wanda turned her phone to him and at first the glare from the window light obscured the screen. He took the phone, turned it, and saw a close-up, flash-lit photo of him and Terry Rogers in what looked like a very romantic lip lock. He stared at the photo a long time. To the unsuspecting viewer it represented a beautiful moment between two human beings, flesh on flesh, the flash increasing rather than diminishing the aesthetics. To the savvy it was oil and water in the same frame, a betrayal of a third party, a political travesty, the Siren's conquest. Gary looked up at Wanda, who had questions but seemed to have answered a lot of them for herself before asking them.

"Photoshop's become so advanced these days," Gary said. Wanda wasn't buying it. Gary knew she wouldn't and knew doubly that Amanda wouldn't buy that or any other dissembling. He hoped she'd buy the truth.

The photo was part of a post in Terra Firma.

What's Wrong With This Picture?

You may not be able to identify the two people in the picture below and you may still be scratching your head when I tell you the person on the right is me and the person on the left is none other than Gary King, he of C2C fame, the target of one of my recent posts. What, you ask, are the two of us doing in the same frame, much less in what looks like an intimate moment? Let me try to explain.

My recent column on the C2C movement and Gary (This Has Got To Stop) elicited more comments from you readers than anything I've ever done. Some of you complained that while I had decimated Gary and the movement in the piece, I was being cruel to someone whom I had known since our adolescence. I took that criticism to heart and I called him up to talk things over. He suggested we meet for a drink. He said, a propos of nothing I had said, that his girlfriend Amanda was out of town. I thought that might spell trouble but I met him anyway.

We reconciled at first but then, after Gary put away a few beers, he tried to defend his ludicrous campaign to put an anonymous blogger in the White House, and things got a little testy. These C2Cers are full of Yeats' passionate intensity but when it comes to logic and practicality they become as temper tantrum prone as a three year-old. Gary didn't have a temper tantrum there in the bar, but he realized his arguments were falling flat, that he was losing the intellectual battle, and that he was way out on a limb I was easily sawing off.

I grew a little tired of this game and was ready to pay up when, pow!, I turned to him and found myself in the embrace depicted below. I didn't realize it had been recorded until I opened my email later in the evening and found this photograph, sent by a fan of Terra Firma who had the wits and reflexes to get the shot. Thanks, Anna P.

I understand Gary is down in South Carolina now, despite his assertions that he is not the driving force in the C2C movement, that it's a crowd–sourced campaign, and that it's about ideas, not personalities. If all that is true why does someone who can't vote in South Carolina need to be in the state? I'll let you answer that for yourself.

I for one am kind of glad he's down there and I'm still up here in Washington. Our evening didn't end with Gary's ambush and I'd rather not wander into some watering hole in the near future and run into him, if you know what I mean. It will be fine with me if we don't meet until *after the current silliness has passed, he has come to his senses, and his girlfriend is back in town.*

BTW, prediction. The latest hippy dippy post from that great god C2C will wake people up to the nonsense that is going on and after a resounding defeat in South Carolina, we'll hear little of Gary or his cohort. Maybe then he'll be ready for a drink and a quiet, adult conversation.

Gary looked up at Wanda. He shrugged, she scowled, the bedroom door opened and Amanda came in, clearly having seen the post and the picture. Wanda left quickly. Amanda gave Gary a phony smile.

"So?" she said.

"I was the one who was ambushed. We didn't plan to meet. She was at the Hog and Heifer before I got there. She grabbed me and took a selfie of us. Look at that picture. How's somebody else going to take that?"

Amanda didn't nod or make any indication she believed him. "She just happened to be in the Hog and Heifer? Terry Rogers? In the Hog and Heifer?"

"Maybe she was stalking me. I don't know. I knew she took the picture, after she had grabbed me and smashed her face against mine, but she said she wouldn't do anything with it."

"And you believed her?"

"No, but I didn't see what she could possibly, how she could possibly benefit from it."

"You see now, don't you?"

"Not really. I think she's jumped the shark with this one. Don't you think this post reads desperate? Won't her readers realize she's gone too far?"

"Going too far is what she does. She's a walking tabloid. I'm kind of surprised you went anywhere near her."

"I told you. I went into the Hog and Heifer and sat down. There was a drink on the bar next to me. She came back from the bathroom and…"

"Gary, come on. Of all the gin joints in this world you just happened to sit next to the woman who'd excoriated you in her blog, the woman who'd given you your first blow job?"

"Swear it's true. You can check my phone log. I've never called her, never got a call from her. As far as I'm concerned it was a random event. For her, now, I'm not so sure. I think I might have been set up, but..."

"But what?"

"Nothing. No buts. I was probably set up."

Amanda stared for a while, to emphasize her skepticism. "And what about this 'the evening didn't end with Gary's ambush'? What does that mean?"

"She needed some help getting home."

"She needed some help? And you helped her, home, to her apartment?"

"Yes. Sort of."

"Sort of? What do you mean by sort of?"

"I... I'm not going to play this game, Amanda. Nothing happened. That kiss was not a kiss and nothing happened. If you don't trust me on this, that's not my problem."

Amanda looked back down at the photo on her phone, then up at Gary. She said nothing. He wanted to say a lot more, but some inner voice, some moral compass, was telling him not to keep going, not to be his own defense counsel. He didn't want to tell Amanda or anybody else what had happened. He was embarrassed about his behavior. Terry had downed a third martini after she had photographed their clutch and her invitations to him became more explicit, when they were intelligible. Gary didn't feel right about leaving her when she was as sloshed as she was and so he got a cab and took her to her apartment building. A couple of times during the ride he thought she was going to throw up, but she kept it together and they made it to her building. It took her a long few minutes to find her keys and while she was doing so Gary, without much thought, pulled out his phone and videoed her, holding the phone as if he were looking at something on it. Once she found her keys Terry began imploring Gary to go up to her apartment with her, to "finish what they had started years ago." She got quite explicit about what she meant by that, not realizing the camera was rolling. Gary declined several times and finally Terry gave up, said she had her friend Mr. Dildo upstairs and she didn't need him anyway, and stumbled through the front door of her building without a wave goodbye.

Gary watched the video the next morning and was ashamed of the fact that he had shot it. It didn't matter that Terry had often resorted to such sleazy tactics herself to document peccadillos. Gary felt unclean even having it on his phone and he erased it without a second thought. Now, with Amanda accusing him of bedding Terry, he probably should have rued deleting the video, but he knew it wouldn't have made any difference if he had kept it. He wouldn't have used it in his own defense no matter what. He had his principles.

"I want to trust you, Gary," Amanda said after a while.

"Then do it."

"I'm trying. But this whole thing has changed you. You know what happens to men when they get power. They think they are above the rules. Especially when it comes to women. Clinton gets a blowjob in the Oval Office and thinks he's safe? What's that all about? Maybe you've succumbed to the same magical thinking, huh? Maybe you did just happen on Terry in the Hog and Heifer but maybe then you thought, hey, who's going to know? I'm bullet-proof."

"You're way off. First of all I don't feel powerful at all. Yeah, I got all this started, but I don't feel in control of anything, don't feel any power. And secondly I am well aware of how vindictive Terry can be and what access she has to spread her lies far and wide. Look at what she's trying here. I knew about that long ago. I'm surprised she didn't turn me in back there in sleep-away camp. And thirdly, there's you. Why would I go out for hamburger when there's steak at home?"

Amanda clucked. "I'm not a piece of meat, Gary," she said as she stomped out of the room.

Gary knew going after her was useless. They'd had fights before. Amanda needed to have the last word so she could go off and think about things without having to do so with a bruised ego. He'd just have to wait things out.

9

"Dad, it's me," Hannah said.

Adam, rousing himself from a deep sleep, fumbled with the phone as he turned on the light next to the bed. The clock said two-thirty-five. He'd only had a couple of hours of sleep.

"You okay?" he asked.

"Yeah, except for every eight minutes or so."

"Contractions?"

"Good going, Doc."

"I'm not quite awake here."

"Sorry. I should have waited. But we're about to take off for the hospital. I just wanted to let you know things were starting and I'm doing fine." The last word was choked off as if a contraction interrupted it.

"Is Jeff going to drive you?"

There was a long pause before Hannah answered. He could hear her puffing out breaths. "No. I'm going to hitchhike."

That was Hannah. That was her mother speaking through her. Had her mother lived, Adam had always thought, the two of them together would have been quite a tag team of jokesters. Michelle always admired Hannah's wit and the way she charmingly handled her father.

Adam went to the window and drew back the curtain. Snow swirled wildly under a cone of street light.

"How's the weather out there?" he asked.

"Buffalo normal. But the streets will be clear. So, Dad. I wanted to call to tell you everything's fine, you don't have to worry."

"Good."

"We haven't talked about it but I know how hard this must be for you."

"No, I..."

"I know Dad. You don't have to gloss over it. You had to be beside yourself. Uncle Mike told me. You lost Mom, you got me, and you blamed yourself. All in one night."

"You knew all this."

"But, it's a little different now. I've had my moments. I've tried to imagine what it was like for Mom. She didn't know what was around the corner. Neither did you. It must have been horrible."

"Half of it was, honey. And half of it was the most wonderful thing that's ever happened to me."

"Thanks, Dad. Dad?"

"Yes?"

"I'm glad you're not here. And I mean that in a good way. I'm glad you don't have to be reminded any more than you already must be."

"Thanks. I'm doing fine. You better get going if you're at eight minutes."

"We're just about out the door."

"Call me as much as you want."

"I will."

"We'll get a flight out tomorrow."

"Why don't you wait on that, Dad. There's a big one coming through tonight. You might get on a plane and end up stuck in Atlanta or something. We're going to be fine. This is our first big deal, you know. We're doing great with it. Jeff's going to be a great dad, just like you. I..."

Another contraction hit and Adam waited. "You get going now, honey. This is a doctor speaking. For the record, I'm calling a boy."

"I'm with you the way he's kicking, but we're in the minority. Everybody else is calling a girl."

"I love you, Hannah. Michelle sends her best. And I know your Mom's with you too."

"Thanks, Dad. Now I'll be blubbering while I'm throwing up."

"That's my girl."

"Call you later."

Adam paced for a few minutes, knowing he wouldn't be going back to sleep. He made some of the room coffee and drank the watery brown liquid quickly hoping what it lacked in flavor it would make up for in caffeine. He thought about calling Michelle but he decided to send her an email instead.

It's almost three, contractions are down to eight minutes or so, and they are on their way to the hospital. H. doesn't suspect anything. She's doing fine. I am too. I must have had a little premonition last night. Just before I conked off I wondered why it is childbirth is so difficult and painful for women. There's no evolutionary reason for it that I can see. So I guess it has something to do with the new. Something new and fresh, something different, never just glides into existence. It has to muscle its way into the world, into our thinking, into our ways of life. Too bad mothers have to take that pain all by themselves. But what's the alternative now? Not having kids? Not allowing the new in all aspects of life to emerge? No way. Thus endeth the sermon. Love you, A.

He finished the email and without much thought at all got dressed and went to his car. He scraped the windshield and got on the street to the hospital. He remembered that he was closer to the hospital than Hannah and Jeff were so he kept his eye out for Hannah's car. When he reached the hospital it took him a while to find a parking space. As he was walking the block from his car to the emergency room entrance he saw Hannah's car, a hand-me-down Honda he and Michelle had given her a few years ago, pull into the drive in front of the emergency room.

He was in shadows near the street and his view was hampered by the fury of the snowflakes, but he could make out Hannah and Jeff as Hannah shuffled into the building. Adam couldn't stop the tears that came, didn't really want to. His beautiful girl, motherless since she was six minutes old, about to be a mother herself. The ghosts of that night thirty years earlier mingled with the snow. The look on Linda Rizzo's face when she told him he had to leave the birthing room, the long half hour in the hallway wanting to burst into the room and find out what was going on, the news that Polly was dead but that Hannah had come through fine. He let it all come and let the hurdy-gurdy of the snowfall dissipate the sting of the memories. Hannah was right. This was going to be different.

He waited until he was sure Hannah had been taken upstairs and he went into the emergency room. He went up to the admitting desk, explained who he was, said that he didn't want his daughter to know he was there, but wanted to find out if everything was okay. The nurse, as he knew she would, said she had no information, that his daughter was in good hands, and that he could have a seat, help himself to coffee. Adam again swore her to secrecy.

The sunrise that came four hours later was a slow coming dawn. The snow was as steady and swirling as it had been the night before. The television in the waiting room alternated between the dire predictions for an even heavier snowfall toward evening and the presidential primaries in South Carolina. He tuned all this out. He just wanted his phone to ring.

When it finally did buzz the call wasn't from Hannah but from Michelle.

"Hi," he opened. "You got my email."

"I did. Where are you?"

"In the motel. I really don't want to tie up this line in case Hannah calls."

"Don't worry. Jeff called the house. He didn't have your number for some reason."

"Called the house? Why? What?"

"Everything's okay, Adam. You've got a granddaughter."

Adam's eyes flooded and his first impulse was to go flying up to Hannah's bedside.

"Everything's okay? He said that? No complications?"

"He said everything went smoothly. I told him Hannah would probably use a different adverb. She's a big one, eight one, twenty-four inches."

"Almost the same as her mother. A girl? I can't believe it."

"She's got a name too, Adam."

"Already. I mean, yeah. What?"

"He wouldn't tell me. You've got to call."

Adam could hardly make out the screens on his phone through his watery eyes. Hannah answered her own phone. She sounded weak. He could hear what sounded like little coos near the receiver. He told Hannah he was so happy for her. He asked what the baby's name was. He heard Hannah fight tears.

"Polly, Dad. I hope that's all right."

Adam didn't fight his own tears. He let them come.

"That's perfect, honey. Perfect."

Ginny had spent the better part of three days hanging out in a student lounge on the Tufts campus with a view of the Medical Center entrance. She felt even more like a stalker there than she had when she was staking out the cubicle in Halligan Hall. Eve Potter, her prey, her obsession, had not appeared, as far as Ginny could tell. After the first day she had made some inquiries and found out that the entrance she was watching was the only one into or out of the building, so she guessed Eve had come in or out at an odd late hour or she, Ginny, had just missed her.

It hadn't taken long at all to get information about Eve. She was active on social media and an open book on Google. She was thirty-two, born in Seattle, studied philosophy at Brown, worked for a year as a researcher in San Salvador, did a post-Bac med school prep course at Columbia and graduated from the University of Cincinnati medical school. She was a fellow in pulmonology at Tufts, not married, seemed to have only female friends, had mourned the death of a cat she'd had for ten years, and lived somewhere in Jamaica Plain. An altogether unremarkable bio. Ginny looked for anything that would indicate political aspirations, any other blogs she might have or had, any indication that she was proficient enough in computer science to pull off the encryption in C2C, but found nothing.

Ginny had called her office at the hospital and asked if she could get an appointment with Eve, but the receptionist had all these questions about referrals and the reason for the appointment and Ginny realized that her plan to confront Eve in an exam room was not going to work.

Gary, meanwhile, was becoming more and more insistent on Ginny's search being successful. She understood his urgency. The South Carolina primary was a day away, he had either been punked or made a huge mistake dealing with Terra Firma, and that Republican nut job Haynes was claiming C2C was in the G.O.P. Ginny told Gary nothing about Eve, in part because she felt a bit foolish in her obsession and her outdated methods of sleuthing, in part because she wanted to keep Eve to herself for at least a while before she was exposed. That is, before Ginny exposed her. As far as Ginny could tell nobody else had come close to identifying Eve as C2C.

Ginny's cold had subsided right on time, on the fifth day, and she was eager to get back to some exercise. People in her office back in California were talking about the warm Santa Annas and the good running weather. Boston was suffering through a midwinter mush season, snow followed by rain, no sun for days. Ginny had taken to leaving the student center every now and then and walking up and down in front of the Medical Center just to get some blood moving.

She was doing just that when she looked up and saw Eve walking straight toward her, head down, concentrating on dodging the packed snow dotting the sidewalk. Ginny had had plenty of time to prepare for a meeting like this, to come up with some line, but she hadn't done so. The two of them were walking slowly due to the conditions but it seemed to Ginny that they were racing toward each other. She said a little prayer, something like "give me the words," and, when they were only a few yards apart and Eve stepped aside to let her pass, Ginny opened her mouth and found the words.

"Excuse me, is your name Potter?"

Eve looked up. Her eyes were red-rimmed and her nose one Rudolph would have been proud of. When she spoke it was clear she was in the grip of a cold.

"Yes."

"Sorry, I don't know your first name, but I remembered the last. At Brown. We were in a philosophy class together. A lecture by, by, can't remember the guy's name but..."

"I took a lot of them. Maybe Sallinger? Logic and Probability?"

"No, but I remembered you because you were really on top of the stuff."

"No. I was just a good bullshitter, I guess."

In her days of stalking Ginny realized the portrait of Eve she was building was a romanticized one, that she was smitten by an image that might be completely false. But as Eve spooled out those few sentences Ginny found she hadn't been all that far off the mark. Eve was, even in the throes of an illness, a cheery sort, easygoing, self-effacing, and, despite the eyes and the nose, beautiful.

"What are you doing here?" Ginny asked, then gestured toward the scrubs Eve was wearing. "I guess you work over there, huh?"

"Yeah. I'm a doctor. You? You teach here?"

"No. Out in California. CalTech. I'm just here for a special project. I should have checked the Farmer's Almanac before I agreed to come out."

"I hear you. I turned down a fellowship in Arizona because I thought I'd see more medicine here in Boston. Boy was I right. I'm in pulmonology."

Ginny laughed and Eve did as well. Her face lit up with her smile.

"If you don't mind me saying, you look like you could use a doctor yourself right now."

"Just a cold. I'm going home, though. I don't want to give my patients what I've got."

"Would you like to get a cup of coffee or soup or something?" Ginny asked, regretting the question immediately. It sounded too eager and Eve clearly needed to be home under the covers.

"I was on my way to do just that. Have you got time?"

"Uh, yeah. But shouldn't you be, I don't know, like sitting in some sweat lodge or something?"

Eve laughed easily. "Alternative medicine? Watch your tongue. I have to make one stop then I can show you a nice little place just off campus. But you probably need to be someplace."

"I actually just finished what I need to do here and I'm not scheduled to leave for a day. I'd love to get a philosopher's tour of the environs."

"I only majored in philosophy because of a girlfriend. Can you believe that?"

Ginny couldn't believe her luck, is what she couldn't believe. Her prey identified the same way she did. "Must have been some girlfriend."

Eve sighed. "She was."

The place Eve took them to was called The Tea Shoppe and was as kitschy as the name implied. But it was toasty, with a working fireplace, and some good eats. The rest of Eve's face flushed with the heat and the steam and Ginny thought she looked radiant, despite all the nose-blowing. Ginny had to remind herself several times that she wasn't just getting to know someone, having a date perhaps, but that she was in the presence of the woman who had the entire country in an uproar.

"So my girlfriend Mika and I went to San Salvador to work on this research project. We were just out of college."

"She was at Brown too?"

"No. Oberlin. She played the piano. She was going to do this year in Central America then go to a conservatory for graduate work. We lasted four months before the government swept in, accused the research team of spying, of all things, and sent us packing. We were doing some good work, work I thought would be very helpful to small farmers and villages. It just didn't add up. Anybody with any common sense could see that."

"Common sense?" Ginny blurted out and wished she'd thought about it first.

"Yeah. Not something in great supply among government leaders anywhere, right?"

"Right," Ginny said, wondering how this could be the opening she was looking for. "The word these days, you know, with the campaign and all."

Eve stared at her and Ginny wondered if she'd blown her cover. But it turned out Eve was only staring because she felt a sneeze coming on. She sneezed, wiped, blew and daubed at her moist eyes, apologizing all the way.

"Are you two still together?" Ginny asked.

"No. She died. We had been back for a few months when she became violently ill with a parasite she didn't know she was carrying. We were camping in Idaho, nobody knew what was happening, and she went in two days."

"I'm sorry to hear that."

"It's the reason I went into medicine."

"Some good came of the death then."

"I guess. I don't know if I'm a good doctor. None of us really do. A lot of us think we're gods but we're just stumbling around half the time."

"Using your common sense?"

"Right. And I better use some now."

"You mean stop gabbing to a stranger and take care of that cold?"

"Yeah, but you don't feel like a stranger. Did we do anything else together but that class?"

"Not that I know of. I wasn't all that active. I had a boyfriend who took up a lot of time, until I realized men weren't my thing."

Eve nodded agreement. "What are you up to now?"

Ginny thought Eve was talking about her search, then realized she was just asking a simple question.

"Oh, you mean this afternoon? Well, I don't know. I thought I'd be working but we're finished, so."

"You're welcome to come over to my place and watch me veg out. Real inviting, huh?"

"Sounds great. I've been around a bunch of wired academics all week. I could relate to vegging out."

"Great. I've got one stop to make on the way."

The stop was Halligan Hall and as Ginny realized where they were going she imagined Eve would leave her in the lobby or something while she went to the cubicle. But Eve invited her through the turnstiles, cleared the passage with the security guard, and, as they were walking toward the computer lab explained to Ginny that she used the lab because her own computer was "hopelessly fucked up."

When they reached the lab the computer at C2Cero was occupied and Eve said she would wait for it to be free.

"Got a favorite, huh?" Ginny asked.

"I've hidden some information on it. Even the geeks here can't find it. Sometimes I think I should have gone into computer science. That stuff, I know I'm good at that."

Ginny had trouble keeping her excitement at bay. Two for the price of one, double your pleasure, the woman of her dreams, an intuitive techy and C2C all in one gorgeous package. The cubicle opened up and Eve took over the computer. She wasn't the least bit secretive about it and Ginny had the feeling that if she wanted to she could stand behind Eve and watch her address the world.

But she stood off to one side to wait. As she was doing so Rob Edelman came into the lab. He didn't see her at first but after a few minutes she felt him approach and turned to him.

"Still here, huh?" he said.

"Yup. All done."

"What brings you to our lab, then?" he asked.

Ginny motioned toward Eve. "Friend of mine."

Rob, looked, saw Eve, looked back at Ginny. "You know Eve?"

"Sort of. College."

"She must run you ragged then, huh?"

"How's that?"

"The work you do. She's always asking questions. I tell her she should take some courses but she says she doesn't have time for that. So instead she takes up everybody's time here. Guys don't mind, though, if you know what I mean."

"She's interested in the guys?"

"No. Not at all, if you know what I mean. But, compared to some of the scenery in computer science, she's a nice eyeful."

So much for gender equality and non-sexist behavior in the STEM world, Ginny thought. Then Eve got up from the cubicle and came to them. She and Rob said hello. Eve gushed about what a help Rob was and Rob blushed at the gushing. They talked about Eve's cold, about a professor both knew who had quit because of some malfeasance and, after a few minutes, Eve and Ginny were walking down the hallway toward the front door. Ginny's phone, in her bag, rang the distinctive C2C post ringtone and Ginny froze. Eve stopped as well.

"What?" she asked.

Ginny took the phone from her bag, looked at the screen, saw that it was indeed a new post.

"Oh," she said, her heart fluttering with the realization that the post came from the woman standing three feet from her.

"Bad news?" Eve asked.

Ginny hesitated. Be honest? Be direct? Ask straight out if she was C2C? Be coy? She didn't know. But she had to say something.

"No. It's a new blog post by, um, uh, C2C."

She looked up at Eve, who was once again staring, but this time Ginny could see the stare came from an imminent sneeze. When the sneezing, blowing and wiping were done, Eve seemed to have forgotten where they had left off.

"I better get home. You still want to play nurse?"

"Why not? If you can play doctor..."

Eve laughed a hoarse, froggy laugh and even though her eyes were rheumy they twinkled.

Ginny decided that to say anymore about C2C might be a red flag for Eve, who, Ginny could see, was not bothered by Ginny's mention of the blog post.

"Sure," Ginny said.

They started toward the door again and as they walked, Eve, through a stuffy nose, spoke up.

"I read his stuff," she said, eyes straight ahead.

"C2C's?" Ginny asked.

"Yeah."

"You think it's a he?"

"Sounds like it, don't you think?"

Ginny nodded and as they went out through the turnstiles, as she followed Eve's bouncing ponytail out the front doors, she marveled at her cool demeanor, her deflecting observation. Ginny knew she was in trouble. She was falling hard.

10

The day before the South Carolina primary it seemed as if every other media piece was about C2C. A judge in the South Carolina Supreme Court briefly granted an injunction of the entire primary before he was shown to have no jurisdiction in the case. The Democratic National Committee had been in secret meetings for days and finally allowed the vote to continue, with write-ins. Amanda's father, Sam, in South Carolina for the meetings, stood behind the chairman of the Committee as he read the DNC's statement. Amanda thought he didn't seem too upset about the whole thing, an indication the Committee had an ace up its sleeve.

The Terra Firma post, with Gary and Terry's picture had only begun to flare up when its rather thin substance was swamped by the news everywhere else that the sky was falling. A C2C win, it was generally acknowledged in the punditocracy, would lead to a Doomsday that would far surpass the chad charade in Florida in 2000. Reporters easily located Gary and his entourage at their redoubt near the airport and soon the parking lot at the motel was packed with a mini-forest of media vans and their transmitters. It was a warmish, bright day, so Gary took to the microphones set up in the parking lot and let reporters ask questions til they were full to the brim with sound bites.

"What will a win by C2C mean for the Democratic party?" reporters asked several times in several different ways.

"The same thing it means for the rest of the country, that we have a vibrant and up-to-the-minute democracy."

"What will a C2C cabinet look like?"

"I don't think there'll be a cabinet. They'll put the laptop right up on top of the desk."

"Don't you think this joke has gone on too long?"

"Don't you think the cult of personality in this country has gone on too long? We're two centuries removed from a monarchy and people still long for a king. They want someone who is dripping with wealth, someone who can fill the imperial void in their lives. But C2C and the people who support C2C are beyond those rather infantile longings. They want a mind and a morality in the Oval Office, ones not connected to any billionaire puppeteers."

This sort of thing went on so long Gary began to lose his voice. Finally he said that the media's concentration on him, not on the things C2C had been saying, was ample illustration of the point he had made originally in Poli-Ticks.

"Read the social media. Talk to the people making the yard signs. Find out for yourself what is bringing voters to the polls in droves. To quote our parents' bard, Mr. Dylan, 'something is happening here but you don't know what it is, do you, Mr. Jones.'"

"What's happening that we don't know," a reporter shouted.

"Ask the Republicans," Gary rasped enigmatically and went back in the hotel.

He had tossed off that last line but when he got back up to the suite Amanda and Wanda told him he might have been prescient. Pinkie and his buddies in the airport had sounded like kids on a lark, but there was some indication by pollsters that a swell of possible Republican write-ins for C2C was forming out on the horizon and might land on the shores the next day as a sudden and surprising tsunami. Chuck Haynes must have gotten news of this because he spent a lot of time in his stumping reminding the electorate that C2C did not want to run for office.

For all the hubbub there was comparatively little frenzy to find the real C2C. No one really believed Chuck Haynes had a route to whoever C2C was, but they didn't challenge him too strenuously. It seemed as if the media knew that revealing the identity of the phenomenon would kill the goose that was laying some very fat, golden eggs for them and their ratings. Reporters and commentators let loose their righteous anger, their bafflement, their dire predictions but you could tell that once they were off the air, away from the computer, they were ecstatic.

Todd Townsend was, of course, apoplectic. His legal efforts to halt the C2C juggernaut had come to, well, naught. President Richards, the man he had bolstered for eight long years, was nowhere to be found, probably drinking to C2C's health and hoping Toad, as he and his inner circle called Townsend in private, would sink under the write-in landslide. Townsend's wife Rita, a striking, razor-sharp Latina lawyer, who seemed to be the brains in the household, lost her cool in front of the cameras at a rally in Charleston and called C2C a *concha de tu madre* before she could be hustled off the stage. Her press officer translated the phrase as "the seashell your mother likes," but the several million South Americans in the U.S. knew it to have a slightly different connotation.

Of all the people in the suite, Wanda was the one who was most interested in traditional politics. A friend of Gary's from their days on the Hill, an organizer of the bipartisan prison reform group, Black Women For Justice, she had been one of the first to respond to the Poli-Ticks post and had done a lot of the initial seeding of social media sites, the boost that led to the phenomenal liftoff. In the weeks since, she and Gary had crossed swords several times over the extent to which the C2C campaign should be led or left to its own devices, literally. In New Hampshire she had begun some serious videotaping and now, on the night before the South Carolina primary, she was doing informal interviews with everybody who came through the suite, including pizza delivery guys. Gary, trying to rest his scratchy voice, granted her a quick few minutes, and said he hoped whatever she was working on wouldn't come out like the doc about Clinton's brain trust in his first election.

"Form should follow content," he rasped.

"What do you mean?" Wanda asked, her eye to the eyepiece of her camera.

"You don't want to do an old-fashioned documentary about a revolutionary moment in U.S. history."

"What would be the form?"

"Uh, just stick the camera in the corner and turn it on, see what happens."

"Dull. Filming is a way to direct the viewer's eye, to show the viewer what he or she has missed by not being there."

"See. It's the filmmaker's personality, his or her eye, that makes a traditional doc. If you really wanted to make a doc about C2C you'd have hundreds, thousands of people filming themselves and their feelings about their vote."

"And who would edit that pile of video?"

"Nobody. Everybody. It would be an interactive archive, a true document."

"It would be like a security camera dump and nobody would ever watch it."

Gary threw up his hands, pleaded voice problems and went back to scrolling through the hundreds of emails that had come in in the past few days. Most of them were either quick congrats and pats on the back or even quicker variations on "fuck you!" But then there was an email from Terry Rogers that he opened, wondering if she might have figured out how to send a stink bomb over the wires. It was short.

We need to talk. I'm not going to be in South Carolina but I need to see you as

soon as you get back to D.C. I'm serious. T.

He didn't trust the email, thought Terry could have been hacked, but he put it in a save folder. She either had some hot information or a come-to-Jesus moment or she wanted to try to fuck up the campaign. But he knew he'd probably follow-up when he got home.

Then, farther down in the emails he came across one that caught his eye. The subject line said, "Help for you with TF." The sender was "securemyass" and the body of the email was simply a link to a video on a blank page site. The video was a security camera image and when he saw this he almost called Wanda over to tell her about the coincidence between their talk and the video. But then he managed to decipher the grainy image and he forgot about Wanda. The camera angle was elevated, over the doorway to an apartment building, a light over the door making the two people standing in front of the door easy to identify. On the right was Gary himself, on the left, Terry. The video was about a minute long and during the minute Terry weaves and flails and makes lewd gestures as she had when Gary dropped her off. It wasn't clear what Gary was doing but, of course, Gary thought it was pretty obvious that he was videoing her. They tussle a little as Terry drunkenly tries to get Gary to go inside with her. Then, clearly pissed, Terry crashes her way into the building and Gary leaves.

Amanda came toward Gary from across the room and he clicked off the video before she sat down beside him. He realized that the email from Terry and the one from "securemyass" were probably related. He imagined Terry got "securemyass's" video as well, that she could make out his filming, and that she was going to sue him for some sort of invasion of privacy (what irony that would be) or sexual harassment or something. But he turned to Amanda and tried to put the emails on the back burner.

"Just off the phone with Dad," Amanda said sourly.

"And the conversation went....?"

"Yeah, it went. South. He said he wanted me to be aware that no matter what happened tomorrow, no matter what happened in the rest of the primaries, there is no way C2C is ever going to be nominated by the Democratic party. He treated me the way he did when I was seven. He congratulated me on my 'youthful enthusiasm' but that like most such things, he said, they were a waste of time. Then I said, 'Yeah, like Operation Desert Storm.' He hung up on me. I knew he would if I said something like that, but, you treat somebody like they're seven and they act like they're seven, right?"

Gary moved over and gave her a hug. She didn't return and pulled away.

"Men," she said, as she stood and went into the bathroom.

Gary realized that the security video was probably enough to get back in Amanda's good graces, but he knew he'd never use it. If there was going to be a reconciliation it would have to come from trust, not evidence. His father had said something to him once about marriages running on faith, not merit. He didn't understand it then, didn't really understand it now, but he thought he caught a glimpse of what his father was talking about and realized it was going to take time for things to heal with Amanda. Too bad her father had to be an asshole at the same time.

Gary looked around the suite. There wasn't much activity, a card game Ed Popper had going in one corner, some television watchers, Wanda trying to interview Ed's girlfriend who, because she was "in film," was trying to direct the interview herself, and not much else. He remembered campaigns he'd worked on in which the night before the vote was the holy of holies, the big push, frantic activity, a major marshaling of all the forces at the candidate's command. But here, sans a bodily candidate or a centralized campaign, things were downright dull. The excitement, he guessed, if there were to be any, was in thousands of homes around South Carolina where people were planning to go into their voting booths and do something they hadn't ever done, most likely; write in the name of their preferred candidate rather than check off a box beside the name of someone ordained by the party. He called Ginny to share some of these thoughts, perhaps hear that she had found C2C, or perhaps get the news she had decided to head back to California.

But Ginny didn't want to talk. Or rather she seemed like she couldn't talk at the moment. She said she had run into an old friend and was spending some time with her. She didn't ask anything about what was happening in South Carolina and she didn't offer any information about her search, even when Gary asked direct questions about C2C. Gary hung up thinking that the ennui in the suite was probably akin to Ginny's mood. She had failed to find C2C. She had made an impulsive trip to Boston and fallen flat on her face. She had probably wanted to triumph and to show Gary how good she was at what she does, but now that looked like an impossibility. He wondered if he should have enlisted her at all.

And he wondered what the real C2C's life was like at that very moment. Was it bowling night somewhere for him or her? Was C2C secretly wandering around South Carolina delighting in his or her fame? Fifteen minutes later he got a partial answer and the sleepy suite of campaigners woke up. There was another C2C post. This one, which Amanda, who had come out of the bathroom to tell everyone there was a post, said was the most beautiful of all C2C's posts, was a short meditation on the birth of the new, on the fact that the new never just "glides into existence" but had to "muscle" its way into the world. It asked why a mother must go through so much pain in childbirth and it didn't try to answer the question. It was a perfect primary eve post. Ed Popper ordered champagne from room service saying with those words they had already won. As they toasted, as reactions to the post went through the roof on social media, Gary and Amanda exchanged a look that he interpreted as faith and he knew that no matter what happened in the campaign, one thing in his life was going to work out beautifully.

"They're all over Facebook and everything, Adam. You haven't seen?"

Adam was back at the motel room after making the five minute trip from the hospital in a half an hour through a building storm. It had taken him almost an hour to decide to leave the waiting room and go back. But he had given himself a talking to and told himself that if anything bad was going to happen to either Hannah or Polly it would have happened already. Michelle had called minutes after he had drifted off sitting in an easy chair in his room, having a celebratory, mid-morning McCallan. He told her he hadn't seen the baby because he was afraid he'd run into either Hannah or Jeff and that's when she said that she had seen Polly and that he could too if he "would get in the 21st century."

While they were talking he opened his computer, found Hannah's page and saw his granddaughter for the first time. She was just as pink and scrunched and oblivious as any newborn. Her mother was disheveled and radiant, Polly already at her breast. There had been no such photographs of Hannah. In fact it had been a day later when anyone thought to photograph the newborn whose mother had died in childbirth. Adam had been so distraught, so guilty even when he had nothing to be guilty about, that the thought of something as frivolous as a photo never crossed his mind. But now here was an array of photos, from all different angles, some taken by nurses, he imagined, a proof and a reproof to Adam, proof the birth went off without a hitch, a reproof to his secret trip to Buffalo.

Shortly after he and Michelle hung up Hannah called. They talked about the photos and Hannah went on and on about what a comparatively easy time she had in labor and how she and Jeff and Polly had all done it together.

"Dad, I know you and Michelle want to come out but not right away, okay?"

"Weather bad, huh?" He looked out at the sheets of white obscuring any view of even the parking lot.

"Yeah, but it's not that. Jeff and I want to get to know Polly without a lot of people around. We'll post every day and we'll keep you up to date on everything but can we say, like, a few weeks before you come out, maybe a little more?"

"Of course, honey," Adam said.

"Are you sure, Dad? I can't quite imagine what this must have been for you and I know you want to get your hands on this little girl as soon as you can, but we're a family here now and we just want a little time. We told Jeff's parents the same thing. They are okay with it."

"I am too. Who wants all that snow without skiing anyway?"

"I love you, Dad."

Adam hadn't expected such a waiting period, but in retrospect he realized he should have. Hannah had never been a captive of her tragic birth story. She had been an independent, self-directed number from day one. She had accepted Michelle as a mother substitute but had always been clear that her real mother was the woman who had died bringing her into the world.

After a few minutes of dealing with his new schedule, checking weather to see when he might be able to get back on the road, Adam realized that he wouldn't be able to leave Buffalo until he had seen his granddaughter in the flesh. He had hardly finished this thought when he found himself, bundled and booted, trudging through calf-deep biting snow toward the hospital. As if in a dream he made it to the glass doors of the emergency room, talked his way through a couple of security points using his hospital ID from Boston and at one point making up a doctor's name, someone he was supposedly consulting with.

And then he was in the maternity ward searching for Polly. A nurse who seemed to be in charge at first thought Polly was in Hannah's room but then pointed to a plastic bassinet at the end of a row and Adam went to it. Swaddled, looking as if she were just emerging from some sort of cotton pod, Polly made a slight move as Adam approached and to him it was as if she knew he'd arrived. Her eyes blinked open and shut and he was sure she could hear him.

"Hi Polly. Welcome to the world. I'm your grandfather."

She closed her eyes again but he could hear her. "What's going on?" she said.

"You're here now. You will be for a long time, hopefully, then you'll go back to the place you just left."

"It was all light, nothing but light."

"I wish you could remember that, but you're not going to be able to. You will when you return. We all do."

Polly wailed and Adam smiled. He wouldn't see her whole trip through life but he had already seen enough to know she was the fitting result of her mother and grandmother's lives. Now he knew why he'd come all the way to Buffalo. Polly, in her words and her wails, was reminding him of the essence of existence, of the brief interlude when we're alive. He could head home now, get back into the world himself, dance with Michelle, do his work, take on any responsibilities people might want him to take, and live fully to the end.

11

Eve's apartment was a small but orderly one bedroom with a bay window looking out on a snow-dusted park. Ginny didn't see any evidence of high tech artillery, the kind you might expect to find in the bedroom of a woman who had eluded some of the best cybersleuths in the world. The pine bookcases in the living room held the usual mix of textbooks and classics, a student's leftovers. There was not much art on the walls and what was there looked almost perfunctory, as if Eve or someone had decided there had to be some evidence of culture in the place.

The little kitchen was homey, though, and Eve, bustling around in it to make tea and to put out some pumpkin bread she had made, looked truly in her element. She and Ginny talked as she moved around, but she kept one eye on her phone and sometimes spent long periods finger flashing through what looked to be a mountain of emails, or perhaps comments on the C2C site. Ginny couldn't help but notice a change in Eve as she did this. She would come up from her session with the phone, try to smile through rheumy eyes, and be somewhere else for a minute or so until she reoriented and rejoined the conversation.

Ginny didn't make any more attempts at including the words "common sense" in the conversation. She could tell something was going on between them that had nothing to do with either

Eve's nervousness about the messages on her phone or Ginny's search for C2C. Eve asked and Ginny told her truthfully about her work, which Eve said she found fascinating. Then they reversed the Q and A and Ginny had a similar response. After a couple of hours like this, Eve said that she had to get to bed, that she needed to fight off the cold. Ginny got up to leave. Eve stood and they were only a few feet apart.

"You don't have to go, if you're comfortable," Eve said. "Sorry I'm punk here but I like having you around."

"Oh, I don't know," Ginny said. "I probably should do something like go to a museum or go skating on the Commons or whatever you do to see the real Boston."

"Sure, of course. Look, those pills I took are going to conk me out for a while. You can stay as long as you want. The door will lock behind you. The couch pulls out and it's all made up if you want to rest. Mi casa su casa."

Ginny's last girlfriend had said the same thing a day before they broke up. But Ginny didn't hear any irony in what Eve was saying. She said she'd stay for a while. Five hours later, with Eve still dead to the world in her bed, after helping herself to some delicious leftovers and half a bottle of a nice white, after bingeing on a Netflix series about an Indian-American comedian, and after lying to Gary when he called, Ginny pulled out the couch, got undressed and went off to a sweet dreamland herself.

In a dream she was following a ponytail all over her office back in California but could never see the face of the woman with the hairdo. She woke briefly during the night to see Eve turning off the living room lights and going back in her room. Ginny woke in the morning more refreshed than she'd been in a very long time. She made herself coffee, thought she heard Eve stirring, and peeked in the bedroom. Eve was sleeping in what looked like a maelstrom. Her sheets and duvet were all twisted around her body, the pillows looked like they had been soaked, dried, and soaked again. Eve's face was flushed and scowling. Ginny thought she most likely had the exact opposite sort of night's sleep from her own. Was it the cold or was something else on her mind?

The morning shows Ginny flipped through were clotted with news from South Carolina and she realized how she had slipped from her stated mission in the space of twelve hours. She was certain Eve was C2C and she still wanted to know how the blog and the deception all came about, but C2C was now a flesh and blood person to her and one she was beginning to care for, to like. She worried that one day she was going to have to confess her sins to Eve, admit that their meeting was anything but random and that she never attended Brown, but that didn't bother her all that much. Eve, she was pretty sure, wouldn't have a big problem with Ginny's subterfuges. After all, Eve was operating under one huge one herself.

The early exit polls in South Carolina were showing a large lead for C2C in the Democratic primary, a lead one commentator called "New Hampshire on steroids." As the morning wore on another story started to eclipse the Democratic primary. A stealth write-in vote in the Republican ranks was shocking reporters and pollsters. One reporter opened his stand-up in front of a polling place by admitting he was flabbergasted by the fact that C2C was giving Chuck Haynes a race, according to exit polls. For the next hour or so the pundits in the studios labeled the exit polls hogwash, a trick, maybe one perpetrated somehow by the Democrats.

"We're definitely in cuckoo land here," one older, growling expert opined. "Give me the days when W. smeared McCain and we had a good old G.O.P. brawl in South Carolina."

Eve came out of the bedroom about this time, looking pale and weak. Ginny made her sit down on the couch, wrapped her up, got her medicines, and made her a cup of instant miso soup, a remedy Eve swore by. Together they watched the news. Eve didn't seem all that surprised by C2C's ascendency in the Republican primary, as if she had checked it all out before leaving the bedroom. But if she wasn't surprised she was certainly more than just interested.

She tried to keep up conversation but kept drifting to the TV and staying there for long minutes.

After a while Ginny thought she heard Eve sniffling and looked over at her. She was sniffling and more, not from the cold but from something else. Ginny let her have a moment, then went and sat next to her.

"Are you okay?" she asked.

Eve nodded but the tears kept coming. Ginny got up and retrieved a roll of paper towels when the Kleenex ran out. Eve finally got some control of her crying and turned to Ginny.

"I'm so sorry. You don't deserve this."

"I'm okay with it. Want to talk?"

"Yes, but I can't."

"I'm a good listener."

"No," Eve said. "I don't want you to get caught up in it."

Ginny did a quick calculation. Put her cards on the table? Hope that her guess about Eve was right? Hope Eve comes clean? Or stay hidden and have to reveal herself sometime later? She took the first route.

"I think I'm already caught up in it, if you're who I think you are."

Eve looked over at her, searching. "Who do you think I am."

Ginny nodded toward the television. "I think you're C2C."

"What makes you think that?"

"That computer, in the computer lab? That's where C2C's posts come from."

"Really?" Eve said, her surprise seeming quite genuine.

"Really. Like the one yesterday. The post came only minutes after you used that computer. I put two and two together."

"Isn't there such a thing as coincidence?"

"Yes, there is. But I don't think that was a coincidence. And I haven't heard you say emphatically that you're not C2C."

Eve stared for a second and Ginny expected a sneeze to follow, but none came.

"Aren't we all C2C?" Eve said after a while. "Isn't that what this is all about? We are part of him, part of his ideas, right?"

"Right. But there's only one of us who posts on the blog. At least I think there's only one. Maybe more. But at least one C2C."

"How did you... I mean, what makes you think that computer...?"

Ginny reached over and put a hand on Eve's shoulder. "I got a call from my friend Gary King. You know who he is, right? He and I go way back. He knew I was in computer science. He asked me to look at the C2C situation and I did. Talk about coincidences, I found out the encryption on the posts was in part one I used as a graduate student here years ago. I came out here on a hunch. I staked out that computer on a hunch as well. And then you showed up. And then the posts came right after you used the computer. And..."

Eve pulled away. "And you didn't go to Brown and you've been in my house all this time on a pretense?"

"I know. I feel bad about that."

"You should. Especially since I'm not C2C."

She said this as forcefully as her stuffed nose and blotchy face would allow. Ginny held her gaze and waited. Eve looked as if she would cry full out again, but held it in and looked over at the television. Then she spoke.

"I'm not C2C. But I'm not going to tell you who is."

"But you do his postings? Is that it?"

Eve couldn't stop the tears then. "Oh, Jesus. Who knows what you know?"

"Just me."

"I don't believe that."

"And I don't believe you're not C2C, so we're even."

"Do you really think I could come up with those posts? I mean, you don't know me but you've seen me the last day or so. I'm not like him am I?"

"I don't think you're far from it. I think you're as lovely as some of those posts."

"Don't say things like that, please. I was really starting to like you. I thought, well, I thought maybe there might be something. But don't say those things just to get me to talk."

"I'm not saying anything to get you to talk. I wish C2C were completely out of this equation. As far as I'm concerned your secret is secure with me. We don't ever have to talk about it again."

"Please," Eve said with more confidence. "That sort of magical thinking won't fly anymore. Look at what's going on. We'll be talking about this for the rest of our lives."

Ginny liked the way this sounded, as if Eve had said "our lives together".

"Okay. Granted. But maybe only to each other."

Eve shook her head. "It's going to come out. You found me."

"I think that was special. Fate, if you believe in that shit. Whatever, something extraordinary led me here. I don't think anybody else is going to follow the same path, make the same connections."

"Gary King doesn't know you're here?"

"No. He knows I'm in Boston and he thinks I was a fool for coming all the way across the country on a hunch. But he doesn't know how beautifully that hunch paid off."

"Beautifully? You still don't know who C2C is."

"No. But I know someone who does and she, in my quick judgment, is quite beautiful."

"That's laying it on a little thick, isn't it?"

"Not from where I'm sitting."

Eve breathed against the tears and smiled a thanks. "I'm so glad it's out. It's been horrible. But I kept doing it. I thought I..."

"Then you are C2C?"

"No. I'm... I'm not. But it's over. It's got to be over. It's done."

"Good. Then you can tell me when you're ready."

"What's going to happen if C2C just stops?"

"I don't know, but it looks like there are no signs of stopping now. God, even the Republicans are lining up."

Eve looked back at the television and sighed heavily. "I know. Oh, do I know."

In the middle of the afternoon the lead story shifted from C2C in the Democratic primary to C2C in the Republican primary. Wanda alerted everybody in the suite to a streaming local broadcast and there Gary and Amanda saw their friend Pinkie, aka Paul Martin, outside a high school voting station, talking with a reporter, a small knot of people carrying C2C signs and singing America The Beautiful behind him. He was less truthful with the reporter than he had been with Gary and Amanda at the airport and claimed that it was the strength of C2C's message that drew him to the shadow campaign. He said he was from North Carolina and that when his state had their primary he was definitely going to write-in "the Republican who can lead us to victory."

"What's our position on this one?" Wanda asked.

"We don't have to take a position," Gary said. "This is a Republican issue."

"But aren't we officially sort of bipartisan?"

"Yeah. At least it started out that way. But in this case it means hands off both parties."

"We haven't been exactly hands off, Gary."

"I know, but I think we can really wash our hands of this one. Let Chuck Haynes be the point man."

"Haynes is saying 'no comment' at the moment."

"If C2C does half as well as the exit polls indicate, Chuck's going to have to come out of his hole."

Gary and Amanda were starting to patch things up, the heat of the primary warming their relationship. They decided to get ready for the night ahead by working out in the exercise room at the hotel. That lasted about fifteen minutes until a reporter found them and hectored them right back up to the suite. Gary and Amanda showered together and ended up in bed, ostensibly for a nap.

"Can we bury the hatchet?" Gary asked, their faces only inches apart on the pillow.

"You mean sweep the hatchet under the rug?"

"Yes. And other mixed metaphors. I want to share this historic moment with you."

"Which historic moment is that? The one your dick is saluting right now or something else?"

"That and what looks like an unprecedented double win by the C man."

"Okay. I'm sort of forgetting what came between us. Couldn't have been that silly picture with what's-her-name."

"Of course not. It was. It was. I don't know. The pressures of the non-campaign."

"So, with apologies to our Native American brothers and sisters, we will bury the hatchet."

Gary thought about a line having to do with burying his hatchet, but that sounded anatomically awful and so he went with initiating a beautiful kiss of reconciliation. Amanda responded and within minutes they were back on track. Then they did actually nap for a half hour and when they came out of the bedroom all shiny smiles the entourage knew they were a couple once again.

"Oh no," Ed Popper said two hours later, looking out the suite window. "I think we've got a repeat of New Hampshire going on."

They all looked out to see a small but growing group of people, many with C2C signs, coalescing in the parking lot, a line of cars snaking out to the service road next to the hotel.

"The question is," Wanda said, "who are they? Democrats or Republicans."

They deputized Ed's friend Megan to scout the crowd and she returned to report that it was both.

"I didn't see any arguments going on," she said.

"Why were the Republicans coming here?" Ed asked. Megan didn't know.

"Maybe," Wanda said, "they truly believe in what Gary wrote. Maybe they are all out there because of C2C's ideas."

"I doubt it," Amanda said. "We told you about Pinkie, right? He wasn't talking about ideas. He was talking about a brand."

"Maybe a brand is the Republican equivalent of an idea. Remember Trump? He was nothing but a brand, didn't have an idea in his head."

In the hour before the polls closed the crowd in front of the hotel grew to huge proportions. Screen lights from laptops and phones dotted the swarm and the cops began to put up tape and restrict access to the parking lot. The line of cars stretched to the Interstate, backing up the exit ramp and about a mile of road. From their sixth floor perch in the suite the brain trust could hear America The Beautiful as an almost angelic choral work and Gary couldn't help get a lump in his throat hearing such human harmony. Amanda, as always, got to the heart of the matter.

"This is not what you were talking about, Gary, is it?"

"What?"

"Them out there. They're here because you're here. They still need their king, har, har."

"Right. Maybe ideas alone will never be enough."

"Watch your tongue. You don't want something like that getting out."

"Maybe I do."

Megan piped up. "I, like, can't say for sure but from what I heard I think they are here because they expect you to reveal C2C's identity if he wins. At least that's what a couple of people down there were saying."

"I didn't make any promises," Gary said quickly.

"You hinted," Amanda said.

"Hinting is not promising."

Amanda gave him a look that said such a comment was beneath his dignity and he acknowledged such with a shrug. But he couldn't shrug off what she and Megan were talking about.

"In that case I guess I'm fucked, huh?"

"No," Ed said. "Haynes is fucked. He's the one who said he had C2C's identity. C2C wins, you go down there and tell the crowd that they should talk to Haynes, see if C2C really is a Republican, really doesn't want to run."

"And we'll be up here watching the crowd rip you to shreds," Wanda said.

Gary looked down. The angels who were singing just minutes earlier now appeared to be ravenous gargoyles massing to stomp his ass.

"Okay," he said. "Everybody on their knees. We're going to pray for a C2C defeat."

No one dropped to the floor but as the first returns came in it became apparent that no amount of prayer was going to stop the C2C surge. In it's very first report on the numbers CNN had both a check and an asterisk next to C2C's name, meaning the network was calling C2C's victory and doubting it at the same time. As they watched the results the entourage could hear the crowd below react to the same news and then break into America The Beautiful. The media was being cautious about the Republican results and for the first hour and a half after the polls closed said there was no clear winner, though Chuck Haynes had 31 percent and C2C had 23. All the commentators said that final results would be a while coming because many voting machines were not equipped to handle write-in votes and those would have to be counted manually. But an enterprising reporter at Politico realized that any ballot flagged for a write-in count would most likely go in C2C's column and thus was able to get a good rough estimate of the way the voting was going long before any of the news outlets could report the figures. His count had C2C nudging Haynes by five percentage points in the Republican primary and swamping Townsend by over twenty in the Democratic primary.

For the first time in a long while Gary wished his parents were not incommunicado. He tried to imagine what his father would say but nothing came, just the sound of a deep and articulate voice, no words. He could hear his mother clearly. She was always the optimist and the cheerleader. She would not offer advice, as his father probably would have, but would have been absolutely certain that Gary could "figure it out" because he had always been a "clever boy." Gary wasn't feeling very clever as the night went on, as the crowd below grew more vocal and rowdy. And he felt downright dumb when a couple of white-shirted captains from the sheriff's office knocked on the door and wanted to know if and when Gary was going to address the crowd.

"We got a real situation down there," the younger of the two, probably in his forties, said.

"Maybe I shouldn't go down then," Gary offered.

"Negative on that, sir," the older one answered. "We'd like to see you address the demonstrators and then we can disperse them."

"And you could help us if you'd tell them all to go home," the younger one added.

"But it shouldn't be about me. I'm not a leader. That's what this whole movement is about. We want an alternative to that sort of top-down leadership. We want a true democracy. This vote tonight. That's what we want. They don't need to hear from me. That would be like politics as usual. This is politics as unusual."

The blank stares from the two captains said it all and Gary told them that he would come down in a half an hour. They said they would see that he got protection and a bullhorn.

The entourage was quiet after the cops left, the TV chatter the only sound in the room. Finally Wanda piped up.

"What the hell, Gar, no time for niceties. You saw those guys, the way they looked at you. That's what you're going to get out there if you talk like you're in a lecture hall. They want to hear a speech, a stem winder, not a treatise. And don't make it seem like you're hiding behind your philosophy. Go balls out. Tell 'em they did a great job. That's all you've got to do."

"That and tell them who C2C really is," Gary said. "How do I go balls out on that?"

"Don't do a Chuck Haynes whatever you do," Ed said. "Tell 'em the truth."

"Yeah," Mark said. "Tell them the truth. It'll be like a piano falling from the tenth floor on your head."

"No," Amanda, lying on the couch with her eyes close, said.

"Don't tell them the truth but don't lie either." She sat up. "You know the distinction. When they ask to see behind the curtain tell them C2C is still getting dressed."

"But that makes it seem like I know what he's up to," Gary said.

"That horse is already out of the barn, remember?"

"Yeah."

The minutes ticked away and then another knock on the door brought two sheriff's deputies, a male and a female, who said they were going to escort Gary down to the parking lot. Gary looked at their holstered guns, excused himself and went into the bathroom thinking he was about to repeat his performance from the Radisson in Concord. But once he hit the relative quiet of the bathroom he didn't feel like throwing up. He looked at himself in the mirror and realized there was no way out of addressing the crowd. And he knew that Wanda was right about the crowd wanting a speech. He looked at his vape pen, lying on the counter, and decided one hit wouldn't hurt. And it didn't until he realized there were cops in the next room. He flipped on the overhead fan, brushed his teeth, swirled Listerine, and went out to face the music.

The entourage followed Gary down the hall as he followed the two cops. The female turned to him as they waited for the elevator.

"I know your little secret, but it's okay, I won't tell," she said.

Gary smiled sheepishly, a small buzz welling up in his chest. "Got me," he said, thinking for sure she was talking about the smell that probably wafted out of the bathroom.

"You gonna tell 'em now?" she asked.

"Now? Tell 'em now?" Gary said, stalling, realizing they weren't talking about some pot smell.

"Yeah."

"Tell 'em what?" Gary asked.

The cop winked at him, took his arm, pulled him to her and whispered in his ear. "That you's C2C." She stood back smiling, looking at the others waiting for the elevator with a proud confidence.

Gary nodded just to have something to do in the awkward situation. Amanda caught his eye and held it, asking, silently, what was going on. The elevator doors opened and they all crammed into the car. They rode down in silence but as they hit the lobby floor they could hear the crowd chanting "Gar-y! Gar-y!" and all eyes flicked toward Gary. The vape had been perfectly timed, he thought to himself, because the sound of his own name being chanted didn't fill him with fear but gave him a lift. Sure, he could give a speech not a lecture. He'd tell them how great they were. And he'd tell them to go home. Easy as pie.

Amanda was in his ear as they neared the front doors. "Remember Concord," was all she said.

Remember Concord. Remember Concord. Gary couldn't extract meaning from the words at first. Was that something a president had said in the past? No that was "Remember the Maine." Concord. Oh, New Hampshire. He was just about to put it all together, that he should not even hint that he knew C2C, when the glass doors swung open and he was thrust forward into the maw of hundreds of shouting C2C supporters who whooped even louder when they saw him come out of the hotel.

A clutch of microphones had been set up, a line of state troopers and cops were keeping people back. The crowd was diverse with regards to age and race, festive in mood, and a sea of signs waved hello. Gary reached the microphones and was about to open his mouth when a lusty version of America The Beautiful began. Gary sang along with them, the pot making him feel like he was at a karaoke night. The weather was warm, the sky clear, the rotating lights of the cop cars were like disco balls, and Gary knew, just knew he could nail this one.

"Thank you C2C supporters! You did it!"

"No! You did!" somebody shouted and the parking lot erupted again. When it quieted Gary stared for a minute, trying to think what might come next. He saw an older woman, maybe in her seventies, who held a bumper sticker-sized sign that said, "C2C For You And Me." That sounded about right. Gary gave it a try as a cheerleader and was blown away by the response, a wall of sound following his lead. Talk about a rush. He raised his hands, lowered them, and the crowd quieted as if he'd turned a volume knob counter clockwise. He was about to speak when Amanda's whispered "Remember Concord" came to him and he got what she was talking about. No intimations.

"How many Democrats do we have here tonight?" A cheer went up that sounded like the whole crowd. "And how many Republicans?" Again a cheer went up that sounded like the whole crowd. "Who needs parties when we've got C2C!" he yelled, the mic's squawking, the crowd going nuts.

And then Gary realized his bag of rhetorical tricks was empty, not that it had been all that full to begin with. He could see the poised reporters all around waiting for him to say something, waiting for their chance to pummel him with questions. And he saw the joyous crowd ready, he thought, not for words but just to celebrate. Crowd or reporters? Who to obey? Without thinking he ducked around the microphones, surprised the cops holding the crowd back and plunged into the ocean of faces.

He had had this dream before, he thought. But in the dream he had just thrown the winning touchdown in the Super Bowl. And he was wearing pads. Now he was vulnerable to the back slapping, hand wringing, hugs and kisses and it didn't take long for him to realize he might have made a mistake wading into the crowd. A burly, bearded, giant of a man gave him a hug that had his spine touching his sternum, then lifted him and swung him around to the great delight of the crowd. Gary was getting dizzy when the twirling suddenly stopped, somebody grabbed his ankles, and in a second he was riding on top of the crowd, mosh pit style. He had been in actual mosh pits and had been hoisted like this and he had learned not to fight the hands keeping him afloat. He relaxed and let himself be carried above the din. A microphone popped up next to his face with an NBC logo attached. He heard a shouted "How are you feeling?" And he yelled back, "Great!"

And he did feel great, for at least another few minutes. He could see stars above. He could feel the hands that supported him as if he were a child being taken to bed. The singing and chanting filled his ears. He wished Amanda was up there with him. He wished the whole world could experience what he was experiencing. Fuck the philosophy. It felt wonderful to be the focus of all the attention. He deserved this. This was his moment.

Then he was aware that something was changing. The chanting became shouts and cries. The hands holding him were not as steady and when he craned his neck to see what was happening he saw a clutch of Smokey Bear hats shoving their way toward him. He realized that he was in the middle of a scuffle, one that seemed to be growing quickly into chaos. The hands below him collapsed and he was dumped back on the parking lot pavement, struggling to stay upright in the pushing and shoving bodies. Cops reached him and almost lifted him off the ground as they hustled him toward the hotel. The crowd had gone from cheerful and peaceful to angry and ugly in a nanosecond. As they neared the hotel Gary could see Amanda and the rest of the suite crew being shoved into an elevator. Reporters were shouting questions from all sides. TV lights were blinding him. He managed to get away from the cops' grips briefly, raised his right hand in a peace sign, and shouted "C2C"! as if he were some political prisoner being hauled off to jail. Camera flashes lit up. The crowd managed to shift from shouts to America The Beautiful and they were in full voice as Gary was moved through the glass doors, through the lobby, down a hallway, and into a freight elevator.

"You okay?" one cop asked and Gary actually looked himself over before answering that he was okay. The cops couldn't figure out who was going to ride up with Gary and while they were huddling the doors closed and the elevator began to rise, Gary the only occupant. He pushed the button for his floor and stood blinking and dazed. It had all happened so fast. He could still feel the crowd's power and energy. He thought he would remember the sensation of floating over the parking lot the rest of his life. His heart was still going a mile a minute. He pinched himself to make sure he wasn't in a dream. But something felt a little off and he couldn't think what it was until just before the elevator reached his floor.

His wallet was gone.

12

Eve had been in and out of sleep on the couch most of the day. Ginny made herself at home, did some work, kept up with the news from South Carolina, took a couple of pictures of the sleeping Eve, made them both a soup and sandwich dinner, and marveled at how comfortable she felt with Eve already.

Eve, however, was both dealing with the cold, which showed no signs of slowing down, and with the news about C2C, and when she'd wake up to find that C2C was leading in the exit polls she became even more distressed. Ginny didn't push for more information. She was thinking more globally. Some force outside the two of them had brought Ginny to Boston, to Halligan Hall, and now to Eve's house. Throughout her life Ginny had rejected religion, her parents called themselves rationalists, and anything outside the realm of the scientifically provable was to be mocked. But she spent a lot of the day thinking about fate and star-crossed lovers.

Early in the evening Eve woke and said she thought the fever was breaking. She sat up and ate the sandwich Ginny had made. They turned on the television expecting the news from South Carolina to be meager since the polls had only closed a half hour earlier. But CNN was calling C2C in the Democratic primary and saying the Republican primary was going to be a close call. Ginny thought it was a time to probe a little.

"You know no matter what you did, you're not responsible for what's happening," she said. Eve stared at the television. "Nobody is really. This is just one of those things the information age is going to have to deal with."

"I could have stopped it all in its tracks," Eve said, still staring.

"But this isn't all bad, is it? I mean, what has politics in our country come down to, money, right? Citizens United, PACs to mask the connection between the billionaires and the candidates, the markets whipping the government around willy-nilly, the cor- poratization of our entire society, secrecy and corruption. We're looking like a swollen banana republic. But this, C2C, this could punch a hole in all that. Look at the result. Not a penny spent and the guy's winning both primaries. Who knows what's next, where this could take us?"

Eve blew her nose and daubed her eyes. "I invaded somebody's privacy," she said. "And it got out of hand. And then I tried to stop it and it got...." She began to sniffle and Ginny couldn't tell if she was dealing with snot or crying. She went to the couch and put an arm around Eve's shoulders. Instead of pulling away Eve nestled in closer and let the tears come. When they had run their course she started talking as if she were in a confessional.

"I sort of fell in love. Or maybe I should say I fell under the spell of someone, though he wasn't trying to cast a spell at all. We met professionally and saw each other infrequently, but when- ever I did see him and heard him talk, I felt so good afterward, refreshed, stimulated. I should have stopped right there.

"But I didn't. His digital self, I found, was wide open, not the least bit protected. I feel really bad about this, but it was like an addiction. I'd tap into his online life, read one of his gems and be renewed. And just like an addict I'd say, 'enough, no more, don't do that again,' but then a couple of days later there I'd be, rooting around in his emails, his notes to himself, even his phone calls.

"And I didn't stop with just enjoying them myself. When he

wrote about Paine's Common Sense it gave me the idea to put up Common 2 Cents. I thought the world needed to hear what this guy was saying, and it also assuaged my guilt a little. I wasn't just hacking his life for my own pleasure. I was doing it as a community service."

She stopped and looked up at Ginny to see her reaction. Ginny's eyes were wet. She leaned over and kissed Eve's forehead. Eve mumbled something about her cold still being contagious but Ginny ignored this and stayed close.

"Then Gary came along, right?" Ginny said.

"Right. I didn't know anything about it until I looked at the site one day and it was being flooded with visitors. I just sat and watched it all mushroom for a couple of days, found out why, and then didn't know what to do. I should have just shut the site down. It wasn't my work, after all, my thoughts, but his. But I reasoned that I had put the site up to share this guy's wonderful world view and why should I shut it down when a whole shitload of people were enjoying it, getting something from it. I didn't think much more would come of it, you know, just a fad sort of, a meme that would come and go quickly.

"And then things got weird and people were talking about Gary's ideas and a write-in vote and I still couldn't put an end to the whole thing. I thought if I didn't have the blog respond to the uproar, if I just kept passing along his words, not have him even acknowledge what was going on, the whole thing would blow over. My bad."

"No," Ginny said. "You've got to stop thinking it's all bad."

"But I kept screwing up. C2C won the Iowa caucuses and then New Hampshire and believe me I spent some sleepless nights trying to decide what to do. I kept hoping C2C himself would recognize his writings on the blog and write something about it himself, but I don't think he made the connection at all. So I figured I'd send Gary and Chuck Haynes an email saying C2C was a Republican and he didn't want to run for office. I thought one of them would find it useful, but I didn't really think the thing all the way through. Now look what we've got."

They both looked over at the television and saw the crowd outside the Columbia hotel chanting Gary's name. Ginny thought the scene looked wonderful. Reporters were interviewing both Republicans and Democrats and it seemed like some political Nirvana.

"It's not about C2C any more," Ginny said. "It's about the idea of C2C."

"I think you're right about that. I mean, how can the Republicans possibly think what he says fits their agenda?"

"I guess it's what he stands for. The Republican rank and file is just as sick of the status quo as the Democratic rank and file. It's really a bottom up revolution, especially since there isn't some hierarchical structure to the whole thing. The cult of personality is so yesterday."

Those words hung in the air just as Gary, on television, came out of the hotel to the microphones. They were watching him live and Ginny couldn't help marveling at the way Gary took to his cheerleading role. Despite what she had just said, she found the fact that her friend was leading this revolution thrilling.

"Wow. This has changed him," she said. And she told Eve how she and Gary had met, how they had had a brief affair, what he was like back then, and how different he seemed now.

As she was finishing this Gary, as if on cue, waded into the crowd, got lifted and carried around. The camera got shoved aside and for a long minute was unable to get a shot of Gary. But what you could see through the lens was the advance of a phalanx of cops, confusion in the crowd, some pushing and shoving and then a lot of pushing and shoving, and by the time the camera got back to Gary he was being escorted back to the hotel, flashing his peace sign.

The whole episode took Ginny and Eve by surprise, as it did everyone else, and they sat silently for a long time. The reporters tried to get their stand-ups done. Cameramen tried to keep equilibrium. And the peaceful crowd turned angry. A woman, whose face and voice would shortly go out to the world as the symbol of the event, screamed that the "state is trying to thwart the will of the people!"

They watched the coverage until the reporters and pundits and commentators ran out of anything useful to say. Ginny and Eve were spooned on the couch by that point, looking as if they were holding each other in response to the chaos they had just witnessed.

"I'm going to have to call Gary," Ginny said. "What can I tell him?"

"Tell him it's definitely gone too far now."

Gary didn't need anyone to tell him things had gone too far. By the time he made it up to the suite, the brain trust was already in full squabble about what to do, how to respond to what had happened. Their first order of business was to try to find out how the whole thing went south. The reporters were getting opposing opinions from the crowd, the cop spokespeople, and the onlookers. Mark, who seemed to be enjoying the chaos, said it was just what happened when you got a spontaneous crowd together with no real leadership. That sounded like a denunciation of the whole C2C endeavor and Amanda reminded them all that spontaneous crowds didn't necessarily have to devolve into disorderly conduct. They were all glad to see that the crowd had finally been dispersed, that it seemed there were no casualties, and no arrests.

Gary watched all this with a combination of fascination and guilt. He was still riding the high of being carried around by those hands, the freedom, the power, and though he knew that all was antithetical to everything he had said and done since his Poli-Ticks piece, he couldn't wash the thrill out of his veins. Amanda saw this and, after making sure he was okay, left him to his own thoughts. Eventually, as scenes from the chaos played over and over on the television, he came to realize that his succumbing to the lure of leadership had, in part, been responsible for both the police provocation and the crowd's response.

"I never should have gone out there," he said finally, and no one disagreed with him.

"It was sort of a group decision, Gar," Wanda said. "Nobody tried to stop you. I thought it was going to be great for my video."

"And I shouldn't have played the shouting asshole demagogue."

Again nobody disagreed. They all did agree that they were going to have to say something soon, but no one seemed to have a handle on what that would be. They didn't know if they should tell the C2C supporters to move on to the Super Tuesday primary states or not. Was that tantamount to inciting a riot or simply good politics? Should they wash their hands of any kind of leadership and put out a press release that said as much? They all knew they couldn't be silent, that the pressure to say something was going to be great.

"I wish we could throw the real C2C to them and either ride him to victory or have him put the brakes on for good," Bella said. She and Vince were taking credit for the Republican side of the equation, though nobody could really make the connection. But all agree with her that a C2C appearance would shape things up pretty quickly.

They watched the news and live streams showing the crowd resisting the police efforts to corral them as Gary was being mosh-pitted around the parking lot. Gary winced as he saw himself looking ludicrous and answering "Great!" to the reporter's question of how he was feeling. The consensus in the room was that the police, the sheriff's deputies in particular, but the state troopers and Columbia cops as well, overreacted to the frenzy and made a chaotic but peaceful scene simply chaotic.

The parking lot outside the hotel had been cleared by the time the brain trust decided to do nothing that night and put out a simple press release the next day saying that the results of the primary votes spoke for themselves. The press release condemned any violence perpetrated by either the police or the demonstrators. It did not mention C2C at all because Wanda had argued forcefully that they didn't want to make it seem in any way that they had been in touch with the elusive blogger.

As they finished drafting the press release a call came from the front desk. A man had found Gary's wallet and was insisting that he deliver the wallet to Gary in person. Gary told them to send the guy up. He was a short, gnomish-looking man, bald with a half-hearted comb-over, glasses, and a threadbare parka. He spoke slowly with a slight drawl and introduced the woman with him, a taller, thin, good looking blonde as "my current." She didn't seem to mind. He held out the wallet for Gary's inspection but didn't give it to him.

"Could I speak to you alone?" he asked Gary and they went in the bedroom. The man sat in an easy chair as if the room was his.

"Thanks for bringing the wallet up," Gary said, sitting on the edge of the bed, wary, not being able to read the guy.

"You're welcome but I have to admit I filched it while you was being hoisted around. Sorry. Had my hands up supporting you and it was right there. Sorry."

"No I'm glad somebody like you got it. I thought it was gone."

"Name's Emory," he said holding out his hand, then pulling it back. "Oh, I already introduced myself out there, didn't I?"

"You did, but that's all right. I don't get names the first time anyway."

"And I'm having a little trouble with the short term stuff. They say I might be on the edge of the big A."

"The big A?"

"Alzheemers, or however you pronounce the goddam thing. Anyway, if I repeat myself won't be my fault, you know. It's all genes."

"Sorry to hear."

"Don't be. Anyway, thanks for giving me a bit of your time. I think I can help you." He smiled one of the goofiest smiles Gary had ever seen. "But first of all let me say I ain't no brain. I'm in air conditioning, repair mostly, some installation, and I'm good at that, but school was never my thing. So there's that right out front."

"We all need air conditioning."

Emory scowled. "Right. Just don't patronize me here as we go along, okay?"

"Sure," Gary said, chastised.

"Anyway, you got yourself in a pickle, don't you? People like me love this guy C2C and love what you're doing, what you did to get his name out. I don't do computer stuff, my current does all that, but when she told me what was going on and when people on the job couldn't talk about nothing else, I looked into the whole thing and, goddam if I didn't feel like something fresh was coming down the line. I mean I don't really do politics either but that's just because I'm not going to vote for some asshole who's dumber than me. But this guy C2C was different and it wasn't just that he was smarter than me but that he was wise. You know that word isn't one we use anymore, but I'll bet my business that's why all them people voted for him today, why they was out there in the parking lot. They want wisdom, right?"

"Right."

"But now that they got the wisdom it ain't enough. They want to see the guy. Me, I'm sorta with you. I want to hear what the guy says, what ideas he can come up with, but I don't care what he looks like. But that's not what I was hearing out there tonight. They wanted him. They settled for you, Greg."

"Greg?"

"Is that it? No, Gary, right?"

"Right."

"Sorry about that."

"That's okay. You sort of illustrated my point. What's in a name, right?"

Emory gave Gary a long, suspicious look, not sure if Gary was being sincere. "A lot's in a name, son. Specially if you can't remember one."

"Yes, of course."

"Anyway, we seen what they did with you, how that ended and when I was out there I thought, that guy needs to find this C2C quick. The Republicans out there was saying Chuck Haynes knows who it is, but Chuck Haynes don't know his own goddam name much less C2C's, know what I mean? The guy's always been in la-la-land. He's a scratch golfer and that's about it. So let me ask you right out. You know who this C2C is?"

Gary ran through a few options before he opened his mouth, all of them some sort of deflection, some variant on no comment. But as Emory held his gaze Gary knew he couldn't lie to such a sincere face.

"No I don't, but..."

"That's what I thought. So what I think you should do is this. You get out there and tell everybody that you're C2C, that you didn't want to say so before cause a your ideas, but you can see now that people really want to see C2C and so there you are."

"Boy, I don't know. That would be a stretch. There are a lot of hackers and whatever who would shoot that one down in a second."

"Backers?"

"Hackers. Computer geeks. People who work under the hood."

"Well, I don't know about that, but okay. Then you go to plan B which is to get someone else to say they was C2C and have them get in bed with those backers and make it look good and ride that into the White House. I'd volunteer myself but my business is having trouble and I gotta keep to home."

Gary realized that while Emory had certainly spotted Gary's problem, he wasn't going to be any help with a solution. He feigned interest, tried not to sound patronizing, took down Emory's phone number and got him and his current out the door a little while later. The entourage had enjoyed the current, whose name was, they swore, Dixie, and who apologized for "Em." She said he'd been having some trouble recently, some medical issues, but that he was a good soul.

Gary thought he was rid of Emory but in the middle of the night he woke and realized he had just come out of a dream about him. The details were few but the look Emory had given him several times, the one of confidence and hope in Gary, unnerved him. Emory was challenging him to do something and Gary felt that he was not alone, that Emory was in fact speaking for all the people who had walked down the path with Gary, all the people who had trusted his vision. Amanda was asleep beside him. He wanted to wake her and tell her how he felt, that he had not been honest with himself. He could still feel those hands lifting him up and what those hands said was, "do something, make a bold move."

The next morning, as they sent out their press release, as they raked through the shitstorm of media coverage of the South Carolina primary and the parking lot incident, Emory seemed perched on Gary's shoulder throughout. Ed Popper and Megan flew out early. Wanda was driving up to Washington with a friend. Gary and Amanda left in Gary's car around noon and were back in Amanda's apartment by eight-thirty, both so wrung out that they were asleep before the end of foreplay.

Ginny Evans had called once while they were driving north and Gary had told her he would call her back when they got to Washington.

"Any big news?" he had asked before hanging up. She had said it could wait. But when he reached her the next morning it turned out that her idea of big news and his were not the same.

"I'm sitting with C2C," she said.

"What?"

"I can't give you a name, address, phone, or anything else but, yes, I've found her."

"So it's a she?" Amanda was in the room and Gary motioned to her, mouthing "Ginny" and "C2C."

"Sort of."

"Transgender."

"No. It turns out that C2C is two people. One of them is the woman I'm sitting with, a truly lovely woman, and the other is, well, not here, somebody I and you and the rest of the world will never meet."

"Why are you going all mysterious on me here, Ginny?"

"It's that kind of gig, Gar. Trust me, though. The mystery is solved, or half of it is."

She went on to tell him the story and Eve's involvement, without using her name. Gary listened with growing excitement until he realized that Ginny's discovery didn't really put them that far ahead of where they had been. Without the real C2C, without somebody who could be lifted above a crowd in a parking lot, they still had nothing. He said as much to Ginny.

"That's your problem, Gar," Ginny said. "We've been doing some thinking here and we think it's best for C2C to just shut down without a word."

"When you say we, does this include the other half of C2C?"

"No."

"Well, don't you think you have to get his okay on this?"

"You weren't listening Gary. He has no idea he's C2C."

"But you said they were partners."

"Let me put it this way. They're sort of partners the way if you plagiarize someone you and he are partners. You get it?"

"But how did she..."

"Not going to go there. Suffice it to say she's an extremely bright woman with a very sensitive soul who identified a person she thought should be more widely appreciated. She wasn't counting on the wideness of the appreciation that you afforded him, but her motives were sincere."

"Sounds like you've fallen in love."

"No comment."

Gary had no comment most of the rest of the morning. He was deluged with interview requests, with lawyers offering to defend C2C in the many court cases that mushroomed almost immediately after the South Carolina win, and with supporters who saw the parking lot incident as some launch pad for Gary to fill in for C2C and claim the title, the nomination. It was all dizzying and crazy but Gary was able to plow through it with a renewed confidence. C2C was no longer a complete mystery. Gary had a way to get to her and that made him feel less helpless. He could, if he wanted to, just shut down the whole operation and walk away. He said as much to Amanda and she asked him if he'd just done a vape hit.

"Gary, it's a lot more complicated than that. I just got off the phone with my father and guess what?"

"What?"

"The DNC doesn't want C2C to go away. They think having him in the race is the best strategy they can think of to destroy the Republicans in the general election."

"Come on."

"Fasten your seat belt."

"People keep saying that to me."

"You keep putting the pedal to the metal. We've got to do some thinking."

Gary nodded. "Where's my vape pen?" he said.

13

The New York State Thruway was clean and dry by the time Adam got on the road. The landscape, where he could see it over the snowbanks to either side, was flat and blindingly white under the cloudless blue skies. It looked like some fairy tale setting and fit Adam's mood perfectly. He felt as if a tremendous load had been lifted from his shoulders though he knew in truth that he had put the load there and could have removed it any time he had cared to. But he had pumped himself full of anxieties for years because he didn't want to put his guilt and fears about his wife's death, his daughter's growth behind him. Now all that was gone, chased away by the sight of a swaddled baby and the fresh air of a new life beginning.

As the miles rolled on, as he passed the spot where he had picked up the distraught vet, it struck him that he had put a lot in his life on hold while he fretted about his daughter. He had been diligent about his practice but not very creative. He figured he had fifteen to twenty years left in his work life and he wanted to fill that as full as he could with good work.

But what exactly was that work? There were the obvious choices, fly off to a disaster area and provide crucial medical services, plunge into the poverty a stone's throw from his home and set up a free clinic, dig into some research that might eventually provide a critical breakthrough that would save thousands, millions, of lives, or just maybe expand his practice, do what he had been doing for almost three decades.

The radio was on in the car and NPR was chock full of news, comment and opinion about the turmoil in the presidential primaries. The details of it all didn't interest him but the very fact of the upheaval gave him a good feeling. He'd always been a fan of Thomas Paine's *Common Sense*, of Paine himself and his scruffy insurrection. All the business with C2C seemed to have the same character. He wished his father, a political junkie before the term was coined, had been alive to see this.

All the radio talk made him think about a nascent ambition he had held in college and medical school, one in which he moved from a successful practice of some sort to an election to Congress and a career as a do-good politician improving the lives of his constituents. But he had realized long ago that ambition was more about pleasing his father than it was truly his goal and he had let go of the fantasy. He had watched a number of physicians take the political stage in the past thirty years and realized that the talents required of medicine were not necessarily the talents needed for a successful career in politics. A doctor's God complex helped with the needed self-confidence, but that was about it. Politics is not science and anyone who has spent their lives at the service of the provable was bound to have a tough time in the realm of the probable, of deal-making, of all the things you had to do to get and stay elected.

The anonymous blogger who was stirring up the whole political scene, Adam thought, might have a good idea. If you were allowed to run for office without all the trappings of the horse race, the celebrity turns, the incessant ass-kissing and toadying to money, if you could simply speak your mind and see where the chips fell, it would be that mind that would matter and the skills you learn in medical school, or any other discipline would translate much more easily to the political arena.

Thinking this got him excited. He saw a new world in which

all that we cynically assume about our leaders and how they came to be our leaders would be buried by an optimism born of rationality. Such a world would make maximum use of the tools we have developed over the centuries, the communication devices, the computing power, all the positive parts of the information age. Adam knew he was being a little pie-in-the-sky about such a future, but he figured he was going to be that way now about a lot of things. He couldn't be bleak about a world his granddaughter just entered.

Was it for him? Could he go back to his youthful ambition, hop on this new train that was leaving the station, run for office in a political world stripped of money, shenanigans, and superficialities? Maybe. It seemed from all the chatter on the radio as if there was already a significant backlash to the blogger by the establishment, as would be expected. But it also seemed as if the groundswell that propelled the blogger's candidacy was genuine, not some PR bullshit, a true upheaval from below.

By the time Adam got to Albany and had heard a couple of hours of the back and forthing on the blogger and the state of politics in the aftermath of some primary wins, he came to his senses. In among the voices extolling both the blogger and a future rich in such candidacies there were older, more conventional voices who seemed supremely confident that their "time honored" ways of doing things would prevail. Not in his lifetime, Adam thought, would he see a political landscape suitable to his talents. But his drive was warmed by a fantasy, one in which he took the ideas he was always coming up with, the notes on scraps of paper, the conversations with Michelle, with colleagues and, sitting in the comfort of his study, not having to be pressing the flesh and downing rubber chicken, he could make his case for office and, eventually, do some good.

This fantasy got him across Massachusetts and only faded when he ran into the snowstorm he'd been chasing all day. Concentrating on the road, turning off the radio, piloting his bubble home, he said goodbye to the fantasy and knew he'd never visit it again.

Terry Rogers reached Gary late in the afternoon, after he had spent the day fending off all sorts of media requests and questions.

"You got my email, right?" she said. Gary said he had. "Well, when can we meet? How about tonight for drinks? I know a place. No pictures. No tricks. And nobody else, just you and me."

"You realize how swamped I am here. There was this primary down in South Carolina..."

"I'm trying to help you. Seven?"

Gary told Amanda he was meeting Terry for drinks. Amanda skewered him with a look, then made the look skewer even deeper when he said she had said she was trying to help him. Gary realized he wasn't going to get Amanda's blessing but he trotted off to the meeting just the same.

The place was a wine bar in Adams-Morgan and Terry was at a small table in a dark corner in the back of the room, sitting behind a large piece of stemware half filled with red. Gary thought she looked a little disheveled, maybe even nervous, as he sat down, ordered a glass of what she was having and settled in.

"Before we start," he said, "let me just thank you for your column about me. I really appreciated getting mentioned in such an august setting."

"I'm just going to say this once, Gary. I'm deeply sorry for that and I apologize. I think you'll see, I'm a changed woman. I'm embarrassed I did that."

Gary scowled. "A tiger changing her stripes? Hmm."

"You have a right to be skeptical. Let me tell you what happened," she said, then paused while the waiter put a matching piece of stemware next to Terry's and left. "I got an email from a guy I've used in investigations, a guy who scours security camera tapes for, uh, information. This time he sent me a tape that starred me as a falling down drunk, in front of my building, trying to get a guy to cheat on his girlfriend and come up to my place. As if that wasn't bad enough, I had written a post about this guy and made it seem as if he actually had come up to my place. Even worse, I had blacked out that night and didn't remember any of it really. But there it was in all its security camera glory and I was caught with my pants not down. Watching that woke me up. I can show it to you."

"You don't have to. He sent it to me too."

Terry seemed surprised by this. "And you didn't do anything with it? You must have shown it to Amanda."

"Nope. I didn't want to embarrass myself."

"Yourself? You were the fucking Eagle Scout."

"Not if you look closely. I videoed you in your drunken state."

"Oh, and you showed that to..."

"I deleted it. Nobody saw it. Especially not Amanda. I don't know why I sunk so low, but I figured your column was my penance."

"You're a good guy, you know that?"

"Only a façade. What was your big revelation? Always check for security cameras?"

"Come on, Gar. We're not antagonists any more. I've seen the light. The security footage started it and then a lot of other things followed behind. I realized that so much of what I've done professionally has been phony, a pose, an attempt to craft a persona, one like Ann Coulter, who is a complete phony herself. She doesn't believe a tenth of the bullshit she slings and I think my percentage was lower than hers. So I went on a retreat."

"A retreat? You?"

"Yup. At a monastery up in Maryland, for a whole weekend, no talking."

Gary took a sip of the wine. "Am I being punked here?"

"I know how it sounds, but I'm being sincere. You'll see. My next column is about my change of heart, about my support for C2C."

"Okay. What meds did they put you on?"

Terry laughed an easy laugh and Gary thought he saw something different, something, well, far away from her Terra Firma persona. A real human being.

"I saw a little clip of you in South Carolina. Not the crowd nonsense after, but before the vote. And I thought, shit, he's speaking from a conviction, he believes what he's saying, he's not trying to be anybody but himself. And that made me listen to you, to go back over the weeks of the C2C phenomenon, the stuff I'd read and written, and I realized I too believe in this guy. Not you but C2C. I woke up the next morning and knew I was a convert, Saul to Paul on the road to Damascus."

"I'm waiting for the punch line."

"Okay. Here it is, but it's not what you think. I want to help you with your dilemma."

"Which is?"

"You can't produce the real C2C."

"You don't know that."

Terry smiled and took a sip of her wine. "I'm dumping my old persona, Gary, but I haven't lost my mind. You're not the type to play coy. If you had C2C's identity in your back pocket, you would have come out with it after New Hampshire at least, certainly after that fracas in South Carolina. So now you're sitting here with a real tiger by the tail, with both Democrats and Republicans salivating over the guy, with a whole electoral process in jeopardy and you're still not producing the headliner. Dollars to donuts you don't know who the guy is."

"Okay. Let's leave it at that. What are you going to do for me?"

"I would hope we'd do it together."

"Okay. What?"

"The guy hasn't come forward yet. I think it's a very good bet he's never going to. Look at the posts, especially the ones after your column in Poli-Ticks. No change, still the same tack, if you can call it that. It's as if he doesn't know what's going on, the stir he's causing, or he doesn't care. So let's just say he's out of the equation."

"Kind of a false premise, but go ahead."

"So you have to create a C2C, bring somebody on board who is plausible, is willing and able to take on the role, and give the public what they want, a body."

"Have you read my original post?"

"I know, I know, that stuff about the cult of personality and all. Don't get me wrong, I'm not whoo-hooing that part of the C2C phenomenon. The anonymous stuff was a terrific launch strategy, but let's face it, at some point there's going to have to be a person to put one hand on the Bible and swear to uphold the Constitution."

"At some point. Who says this is the point?"

"I do. Have you been reading the newspaper recently? Things are getting very, very complicated. Remember what happened <u>after</u> they stormed the Bastille? We may have seen all the revolution we're going to see in this matter. C2C has become much, much more than the sum of his posts. Other forces are going to take over, are already taking over. You've got to stay ahead of the curve, be proactive before the steam runs out of the phenomenon."

"And what would be wrong with that?"

"Huh?"

"If the C2C bubble bursts?"

"Well, you lose."

"Lose what? Haven't we already won?"

"Gary. You finally get the best looking girl in your high school to go out with you and you stand her up? Is that what you're saying? Maybe I just have the zeal of the convert and you're jaded already, but if C2C just goes poof because you can't produce the real person behind the whole thing, it's the country that loses, democracy that loses. Don't get lost in your purity. You've done a marvelous thing for America already. You got the guy from first to second to third. Swing the bat. Get him home."

"With a phony C2C?"

"Not phony. An embodiment. Arthur Miller writes a great character, Willy Loman, and he decides that because there's no real Willy Loman, he'll just trash the play. What a tragedy, right? No, Arthur Miller puts a human being in the Willy Loman role and we're all much better off for it. Gary King creates a fiction of sorts as well, an anonymous guy who stirs the soul of a nation. Then he trashes his creation? I don't think so. I think he casts the role. We talk about political theater. Isn't the logical extension of that finding someone to play one of the greatest political roles our nation has ever seen?"

"Who are you proposing to cast?"

"We'll work on that."

"We. What's your part in this?"

"I get the exclusive. I get credit for finding the true C2C."

"You realize of course that the cybersleuth world is going to be down your throat in a nanosecond."

Terry tilted her head coyly and broke into a sly grin. Gary scowled, not getting the joke.

"Down my throat?" she said.

"I thought we were being serious here?"

"Sorry. I am dead serious. It was just a, well, seminal moment for me." She cracked up at her own pun and Gary couldn't help laugh with her. Was she fun back then, other than in an obvious way? He couldn't remember. The layers of muck since had obscured any trace of lightness, but maybe she had been different, maybe she had taken on a public persona that had nothing to do with her true self.

"Okay, well, you've got to realize I'm not going to, uh, jump in bed with you because you claim to have had a change of heart. And I don't think producing a faux C2C is the way to go. But I'll be happy to continue the conversation when I see your, what would you call it, mea culpa column?"

"See how much in synch we are. That was exactly what I was going to call it. But you're not playing fair. Do I just say I've had a change of heart and I now support C2C?"

"Yes. Right. Then we talk."

"But how do I deal with the eight-hundred pound gorilla in

the room? What do I say about the fact that C2C is still a no-show?"

"Nothing. Don't even mention it. So far it's something of a non-issue. The voters have believed in him and that's enough. Period."

"Pretty unrealistic, isn't it?"

"That would be fitting. Your readers are going to be scratching their heads anyway, wondering if they overslept, if it's already April Fool's Day."

"Don't worry. They'll know I'm sincere. You can't give me some sort of commitment?"

"One teenage blowjob and you want commitment?"

"That hurts. Wasn't it more than just one teenage blowjob?"

"Yes, but still not enough for commitment. Write the column and we'll talk."

"I expected a little more from you. I want to know that I'm not going to hang my ass out and then be left all by myself. I thought you'd be glad to have someone like me, someone who doubted the whole phenomenon and who did a 180, who could give the whole thing real creds, and you'd be a stand-up guy about sharing the solution to the problem."

"But I don't know who the stand-in would be. Do you?"

"No. I think that's your choice. You've got that woman at Cal-Tech working with you. She can take care of the cyber world, right?"

"How did you know about her?"

"Gary, please. Give me a little respect, huh?"

Gary bit his lower lip and swirled his wine. He didn't trust what he was hearing but he didn't exactly distrust it either. Her angle seemed transparent enough. She wanted to contradict herself without ruining her brand. She was clearly hopping on the bandwagon, but even as successful as C2C had been so far, she didn't need to do so. She could maintain her opposition and score just as many points with her audience as she might changing her mind. And certainly the Republican part of the puzzle had something to do with that alleged change of mind. But he couldn't see a downside for him, for the campaign if he threw her a small bone.

"All right. You write your column and we will sit down with my little brain trust and try to figure out if we can pull a rabbit out of an empty hat."

Terry smiled, reached across the table, and when they shook hands, hers lingered in his just a little bit more than was necessary. He would remember that, he thought, in case anything went awry later.

14

Gary expected Amanda to be waiting for him like an eager puppy, ready for the news from his meeting with Terry, but he found her hunched over her laptop, pecking away. She didn't look up when he came in the bedroom.

"Give me a sec to finish here," she said. "You see the news?"

Gary said he hadn't, then did a quick check of his key sites and saw that the Democratic National Committee had made their move. "After careful consideration of the current situation, we have decided that we will allow the votes in the primaries, those which have finished and those to come, to stand." All to the good, Gary, thought, and then got to the "but" part of the statement. "However, because we affirm the necessity of having an informed electorate and because we feel a key part of informing that electorate is the debate schedule we have arranged, we are making participation in the next debate, the final debate of the primary season, mandatory for any candidate seeking the presidential nomination from the Democratic party."

There was no mention directly of C2C. There didn't have to be. Amanda finished what she was doing and turned to him.

"Remember I said my father didn't look bothered by that news conference last week?" she said. "This was the ace up their sleeve."

"What's the response been?"

"Guess."

"Outrage. Threats of violence. Acquiescence. I don't know."

"All of the above. But the main thread seems to be a call for C2C to come out of the shadows and take his place at the debate."

"Sounds like my night has a theme."

"How did things go with the holy terror? Let me check. Lipstick on your collar?"

Gary told her about Terry's alleged change of heart and got the snort out of Amanda he had predicted on his ride home. Then he told her about Terry's plan to put a phony C2C in front of the public. Amanda had the same questions about the scheme Gary had. As they spoke Gary could see his inbox filling, his phone ringing continuously. He saw a call from Ginny come in and he took it.

"I'm about to get on a plane, but I wanted to touch base with you," she began.

"Any news on your end?"

"I've got a new girlfriend."

"Great. Have a good flight. Talk to you later."

"Funny. What's the plan? How are you going to work this new requirement?"

Gary switched to Face Time and saw Ginny in line moving toward a jetway. "I don't know. Remember, I'm not in control here. I bet there are lawyers ready to challenge the ruling. And Amanda says there seems to be a call for C2C to show himself. But..."

"Get off Face Time, Gary. It's not secure," Ginny said, and waited until they were back to a regular call. "Do you think you'll want C2C to say anything? We have decided to shutter the whole operation."

"We? Girlfriend?"

"You're really quick, Gary."

"Sorry. I just came from a chat with Terry Rogers."

"Of Terra Firma fame?"

"Yes."

"Are you in one piece? Is she?"

"Yes. But she was somewhat prescient about the DNC news."

"Prescient or she knew and didn't tell you?" Ginny said. Amanda, who was close enough to hear both sides of the conversation gave this a thumbs up.

"I'm not going down the road to paranoia."

"I think you should. Anyway, what did she say?"

"A few things but most importantly that we should put a phony C2C in front of the public."

"Does she know about me, about what I've done up here?"

"She knows about you but I don't know if she knows about what you've done."

"Well how could she think about faking C2C's identity if she thought he was in control of Common 2 Cents and could easily embarrass us if we tried to give the public a fake C2C?"

"Her answer was that if he hasn't come forward so far he never will."

"I've got to go. I'm in my seat."

"Okay. One question. Can your friend shut down the site completely, leave no trace?"

"She can shut it down but nothing on the Internet can be gone without a trace. There's a chance somebody in the future could find a trail we hadn't thought of and reconstruct it all. But, the answer to your question is a qualified yes."

"How academic of you. I'll call you tomorrow. You're not going to shut C2C down right away are you? It could be valuable in the next phase of this shit."

"No. We'll keep it up for a while."

"Good. And congrats."

"On?"

"Solving the mystery, finding a new girlfriend."

"Kind of scary, isn't it?"

"Scary?"

"Too improbable. I'm going to give my grad students the problem, see if they can determine what sort of odds we beat."

"I think this one's beyond math, Ginny."

"Nothing's beyond math, Gar. Bye."

Terry Rogers put out her new post only hours after she and Gary had met.

Mea Culpa

As you can tell from the title of this column, I need to make an apology. First, to Gary King and Amanda Tompkins. I stepped over the line in my last post and I am sorry for that. Secondly I need to apologize to all you readers who have followed me in my campaign against the write-in campaign for C2C. I have changed my mind about this whole phenomenon and what it means for our democracy today. Like many of you the idea of a faceless candidate was so new to me that I reacted to it without thinking. I have now come to believe that a candidate represented only by his or her ideas is not only possible and legal in our system but is very healthy for the electoral process.

Up to a point, that is. What we have seen so far is a candidate who has introduced himself to us through blog posts, through ideas and philosophies, and I, for one, think that this has been an excellent way for us to get to know him. One of the reasons that C2C's appearance has been so jarring for the country is that he is so far ahead of the curve. We are contrasting him with the other candidates who are, of course, still operating in a paradigm that has been in place for centuries, and so even people like myself, professionals whose lifeblood is the political process, missed the significance of C2C's ascendancy.

But as we all know a faceless candidate is quite different from a sitting president. A candidate can, these days, reach voters through a variety of platforms that are not stages. His or her physical presence is not required. But in order to govern a president needs to be in rooms, on television and media, at international meetings and involved in the thousands of real world things a president is required to undertake. And so, while I am fully in favor of the C2C brand of campaigning so far, it is time for the world to get to know the person behind the prose.

As I have said many times my contacts and investigative avenues are vast, and, sure enough, they have delivered to me the identity of C2C. We have spoken and I have agreed not to reveal his identity here, but both of us will be present at a press conference in the next few days. As always in my bipartisan way I will not be endorsing the candidate but will simply be providing a service for the country. See you then.

Needless to say, the post caught Gary and the rest of the world by surprise. Gary was having one of the best sleeps of the past few weeks when Wanda woke him and told him about it. Gary then tried to reach Terry but she wasn't picking up and texts to her went unanswered.

"I feel like a fool," Gary said to Amanda later in the morning. He had been deluged with emails, Facebook posts, tweets, media requests upon media requests and phone messages that clogged his voice mail in minutes.

"That's kind of accurate," Amanda replied.

"What do you mean?"

"Why did you even think that woman would have a real change of heart? All she's had is a change in strategy."

"I take it back. I don't feel like a fool. I did tell her I wasn't committing to anything before I saw her mea culpa post."

"Yeah, well she just gave your lob an overhead smash. What's the next move?"

"Good question. She hasn't got the real C2C. We know that. But she's clearly got somebody and she's clearly not afraid of being exposed. Which means she's confident I'm going to go along with her choice. And why is she confident? Because if I do otherwise, I'll have to prove my case by producing the real C2C."

Amanda heard this but was busy with something on her laptop. "Good," she said. "They haven't taken down the Common 2 Cents site yet. Get on the phone and tell Ginny we might need it to stay up."

"I already did."

"Good going."

Gary realized that a rebuttal on Common 2 Cents would be a

very last option, if one at all. Terry, in her devious and dishonest way, had framed the argument. Was a candidacy built solely on ideas viable right through the nominating process, into the general election, or was it now the time for the candidate to reveal himself?

"Be practical," Wanda said when they talked the next day. "It's time to convert all this C2C energy into support for an electable candidate."

"Have you been reading the comments, tweets, everything?" Gary said.

"No, Gary. I've been doing my nails for the last forty-eight hours. I know what the trending sentiment is. Hold the course. Who needs a body? That kind of stuff. Fuck the DNC. But we can't fuck the DNC and expect to get our guy elected. There are rules, laws. It's time to play their game."

"That's what's killing me."

"What, growing up?"

"You really think that?"

"Yeah, sort of. Did you ever see this as anything but a lark?"

"Of course I did. Do. I mean the DNC's insisting on a candidate's physical presence at the debate? That can be challenged. What if there were a candidate who, for some reason, couldn't make it to the debate? A handicapped person, say. They wouldn't deny him or her the nomination because of that. They would set up some video system or something so the candidate could participate. Well, why won't they do that for C2C? They could arrange for a way for him to text in if he cared to. If he doesn't text in it doesn't mean he isn't there. You see?"

"I see a desperate man."

When Gary got home, Amanda gave him two pieces of news. First, Terry had posted a time and place for the news conference: the next day at the National Press Club. She was doing it up in style. Secondly, Amanda's father Sam had once again invited them out to dinner that night.

"I said we'd go. That all right with you?"

"Dandy. What's he going to do, crow about his coup?"

"Probably. You've got to admit they came up with a good solution to their problem."

"Yeah."

Gary started to walk into the bedroom. "What did Wanda say," Amanda asked.

"Told me to grow up."

Amanda went to him and gave him a hug, "You're all grown up, Gar. It's the country that's still in its adolescence. We're not dead here yet. Get that fucking Terry on the line and tell her to grow up."

Gary returned the hug and they stayed like that for a long while. Gary went back to the beginnings, to a dashed off treatise meant to impress Amanda, to show her that he was employable. If it had ended there would things have been better for him? For them? Maybe, but he'd probably still be unemployed and trying to decide what to do with his life. C2C had given him not only a purpose but a reputation as well, one he was sure would pay off for many years to come. So, why be a wimp in all this? Why not stand up for a principle until they knock you down? He gave Amanda an extra squeeze. He was back on track.

"So, good time to talk about our future?"

Amanda pulled away from him a little and smiled.

"You know what I like about you?"

"What?"

"Your sense of timing."

Gary cocked his head. "You're being ironic, right?"

"Yup."

Ginny got in touch with Gary just as he and Amanda were going out to have dinner with Amanda's father.

"My friend is really worried," she said. "C2C may not have been what she intended when she started the blog, but it is her baby and she's not too keen on having somebody else pretending they're C2C."

"I bet," Gary said. "That's why I said she should keep the blog open, in case she needs to counter this move by Terry."

"But she worries she's going to be more vulnerable like that."

"You guys have got things encrypted well still, right? If nobody but you has gotten through yet, what's going to change?"

"Do you know how many people knock on her cyber door every hour, every minute? She keeps telling me, 'You're living, breathing evidence of my vulnerability.'"

"No wonder you fell in love."

"I'm serious, Gary. If things get blown open, if someone makes the connection between her and C2C, if the real C2C finds out, her reputation would suffer."

"I know about that one. We're on our way out to meet with Amanda's Dad, who is on the Democratic National Committee. If I get any new intel I'll let you know."

They met at an even more upscale place than their last dinner and Sam seemed much more buoyant than he had. He extolled the virtues of the kitchen, ordered a very expensive bottle of wine, and banned talking about C2C until they had enjoyed their meal. Amanda skirted that by admiring his new tie and telling him he looked great despite the recent events. He thanked her but they didn't get around to C2C until dessert.

"Okay. So that was one of the better lamb chops I've had in my life. I'm ready to talk. How are you guys handling this news conference tomorrow?"

"How are we handling it?" Gary asked. "We don't have anything to do with it. We're as much in the dark about it as you are?"

The grin that came over Sam's face reminded Gary of the bad guy's smirk in many a Western, the one the character usually delivered with a pistol in his hand.

"Well, I'm not really in the dark."

"You know who the real C2C is?" Amanda asked.

"I know who's going to be introduced, tomorrow, if that's what you mean."

"And how did you come about this knowledge?" Gary asked.

"How? I can't really say."

"You don't really have to, do you?" Gary said. "There seems to be only one route into the information."

"Terra Firma?"

"Right."

"Maybe. Let's not talk about how one comes into information in this town. You two are young. Someday you'll understand the back alleys. But for now you don't have to. But as far as tomorrow is concerned, you do have to be prepared."

"I've been trying to do that but your friend Terry has been, uh, too busy it seems to get back to me."

"Not really my friend. Wouldn't trust her to babysit my goldfish. But you've got to respect her tactics, her acumen."

"Why do we have to be prepared, Dad?"

"You're going to be there, right?"

"Yes," Amanda said.

"Maybe," Gary said.

"No maybes. You definitely should be there. And you should be prepared to go with the flow. There are going to be some real questions about why you did what you did and why you didn't reveal C2C's identity earlier."

"And how about if we say we didn't reveal C2C's identity earlier because we didn't know it earlier and we don't know it now," Gary said.

"Then you're going to look pretty clueless."

"Not if a few mouse clicks after the press conference is over the fact-checking cyber world declares the revelation a fraud."

"What do they know? They say, 'Hey this isn't your guy,' and the C2C supporters say, 'How do you know? You haven't found him yet.' Maybe the key to finding him wasn't in the code but in something like intuition."

Gary didn't like the sound of this. He looked over at Amanda, who was staring at her father, probably reading the same, if not more, into what he was saying.

"Okay," she said. "Everybody accepts this C2C and you know

who it is and you're saying we have to be prepared to swallow the party line, literally. What should we say?"

"'Manda. You haven't asked me a question like that since second grade. You want me to tell you what to say?"

"Give us a first draft. We'll modify it at our leisure."

"Come on, honey. I hear some anger in that voice. I'm proud of you, proud of what you two have done. I was pissed of course, at first, but I have to give you credit. You've done the country a great favor. Entre nous, Todd Townsend's a horse's ass. You've dethroned him and you've got Chuck Haynes sputtering over in the corner. Brilliant stuff. You'll get due credit, if you play your cards right."

Gary sighed heavily. "Congressman, I mean no disrespect but you're making this all seem like it's a *fait accompli* is coming off as truly patronizing. Put your cards on the table, please, and then we'll see how to play ours."

"My cards are the nation's cards, Gary. The Democrats need to hold the White House, especially since there's a good likelihood that we'll be picking up four more seats in the Senate in November. I want to see a united party come out of that press conference tomorrow, a party that can stand behind C2C and ride this enormous wave of support for him, or her, into the election. And one way we can insure that happens is if you two, at the center of the C2C campaign, refrain from any speech or actions that would disrupt that unity."

"Whoa," Gary said. "I'm no lawyer but that sounds suspiciously like prior restraint."

"It's restraint, I'll grant you that. But it's you who will have to be doing the restraining. You'll have to stuff your egos and bruised feelings and tell the good people of the media just why you didn't reveal C2C's identity earlier."

"And why was that, Dad?"

"You were young. You got the whole thing started and you didn't know how to end it. C2C was confused as well. And now that Terry Rogers has scooped the entire world, you're glad to tell

everybody about this wonderful candidate and support the candidacy."

"And if we think the candidate Terry's dogged investigation
has coughed up is a drooling disaster," Gary said, "do we still sing
his praises?"

"He won't be. He isn't. Or she isn't." The smirk came again and
Gary looked down to see if Sam had a pistol under the table.

They didn't get much more out of Sam, even when Amanda
did some pouty thing from her teenage years that had always
worked before. They walked home from the restaurant chewing
the whole thing over.

"Maybe we just don't go," Amanda said. "We can say it's not
in our hands now, never was, good luck."

"That would be the smart thing to do, I guess."

"But that's not what you're going to do, is it?"

"Probably not. I haven't done the smart thing a lot recently. I
should be consistent, I guess. Plus, if they are going to shred my
golden idea I would like to be there to pick up the pieces and give
it a proper burial."

"Think quite a bit of ourselves, don't we?"

"Yes. Yes I do," Gary said, looping his arm over Amanda's
shoulder as they walked. "I remember a professor telling me that
political idealism was an oxymoron. It doesn't feel that way to me.
The C2C campaign has been motivated by ideals throughout and
look at how that's played in the political realm. You've got one of
the two major parties in the country stooping to fraud in order to
try to finesse the product of our political idealism. And from what
your father says they still need us to validate that finesse, to bend
a knee to the tired and cynical way we elect leaders in this country.
I don't want to watch that on TV. I want to be in the front row."

Amanda surprised Gary when they got in the front door of
her apartment, whipping off her clothes, helping Gary with his,
almost dragging him into the bedroom and leading them into a
wonderful fuck.

"Is this all because of my idealism?" Gary managed to ask as they rolled happily around on the bed.

"It's not your buff body, Gar," Amanda said.

"That hurts."

"That doesn't," Amanda moaned. "Keep going."

15

The news conference was being held at the National Press Club, in one of their bigger rooms, one with a viewer's balcony. Terry was sparing no expense to trumpet her triumph. But the room wasn't nearly big enough to hold the crush of media and civilians who jammed the elevators and the entire lobby of the building before being let in.

Gary and Amanda waded into this crush and quickly became its focus. They "no commented" their way through the bodies, cameras and microphones, were given special treatment as they took the elevator and walked to the conference room, and then were ushered to a front row seat. A podium had been set up and a newly minted sign with the Terra Firma logo was pasted to the front of it. The National Press Club logo backdrop was impressive and Gary stared at it for a while. The room seemed to reek power and politics. He felt as if he were in enemy territory. Wasn't a room like this, a press conference like this, the very thing he was indirectly railing against when he wrote his essay? And here he was supporting the establishment, showing up at a sham event. He looked around almost as if he were seeking an exit. An array of camera lenses bristled from the back of the room. There was no sign of Terry. A very young looking radio reporter, a guy with spiked-up hair and camo jeans, sat next to Amanda and introduced himself. Amanda pointed to his microphone and held up her hands. He said it wasn't on. She smiled politely and turned back to Gary.

"See my Dad yet?" she asked.

"No, and I'm not sure I want to," Gary said. "We had enough of his gloat last night."

Amanda sighed. Then it became evident that something was about to happen. The buzz in the room quieted and Gary could hear Terry's voice cut through the new quiet. She reached the little stage accompanied by a tall man in a dark blue suit, middle-aged, who looked like he'd been feeding from the trough of the financial markets for a number of years. He was tanned and patrician, quite presidential looking. He and Terry stood to the side of the podium and simply faced the packed room. Their whole demeanor, the little smiles to each other as the cameras went explosive, said, "This is the guy."

Gary's stomach clenched. The image of Terry's choice was one he had been seeing in nightmares for months, a powerful insider who might be able to mimic C2C's words but could never match his soul. Gary knew then for certain that he had failed, that his lack of Washington savvy had done him in. He could hear the reporter next to Amanda cooing into his microphone about "this modern-day coronation." Gary thought it might be rude of him to puke all over the National Press Club's fancy rug, but that was what he felt like doing.

Then the man took the podium. He seemed quite comfortable behind the bouquet of microphones. He waited, smiling, for the room to settle, for the shutter storm to subside. When it finally did he gave his name, Aaron Caseworth, and spelled it out, as if he'd done this sort of thing before.

"I have been a C2C supporter since the very beginning," he said, a broad smile appearing on his face as if it had just been badly Photoshopped there. The room chuckled with him. Of course you have. You are he. "I know, as you do, that Terry has not always been a supporter but it is so edifying, so welcoming to see a journalist who is flexible enough to alter her opinions when the facts become clear." He turned to her as if he were giving her an award. "Welcome to the movement, Terry." There was a smattering of applause and he turned back to the microphones.

"It is my great pleasure to be here today. When Terry asked me to come I didn't hesitate. I was quite comfortable with C2C being both anonymous and the focus of a movement, but the time is right for him to move into the arena as a full person." He pointed to Gary and continued. "And thanks of course to Gary King, whose vision ultimately brought us all here today. Thanks, Gary."

Gary nodded but he would have preferred rushing the stage with a couple of cream pies. He was boiling. The more Caseworth talked, the slicker and slipperier he sounded. The thing that hurt the most was that Gary, and he assumed the rest of the world, could easily see this guy speaking from the Oval Office, glad-handing crowds, schmoozing bankers and legislators, in other words, being presidential. He was so business-as-usual in Washington it hurt. He was a disaster.

"Now, it's my privilege to introduce to you a woman who truly needs no introduction in this town. She is fearless, forthright, dogged, and did I mention she was fearless? As the rest of the country was trying to find C2C, she was digging even deeper, trying to find out for herself and her readers what was behind the phenomenon that has been sweeping the country for almost two months now. And when she found that kernel, she also found the real C2C." Again the plastered-on grin, again the room filled with a cacophony of shutters. "Terry, come up here. This is your party." He winked at that and the cameras ejaculated again.

Terry gave him a fist bump as she switched places with him. Gary could sense a shift in the room's balance. The seasoned reporters were scowling in their seats. The protocol was off. The order of appearance at the mic was reversed. Terry should have gone first and introed Caseworth. Was Terry just a neophyte or was something up? She didn't look rattled. In fact she looked terrific in a pants suit that draped beautifully and her signature two-buttons-opened silk blouse.

"Thank you, Aaron," she began. "I asked Aaron to share his accomplishments with you but he declined, as you might suspect. Google him, people. You will be surprised by the depth of his commitment to this country."

She led a little applause and then turned back to the mics. "But we're not here to talk about Aaron, or about me, are we?" She looked carefully at the crowd, listening, it seemed, for the sounds of confusion. She got some and smiled at them. Then she continued. "No, we're here to talk about C2C. I don't need to give anyone in this room any background on this wonderful phenomenon that has been with us for the past two months. You have all the information you need on that score. Except, of course, for the identity of the person behind the whole thing, the star of the show. And so, without further delay, I want to introduce you to the real C2C."

Again she waited. Caseworth, the room now realized, had been one of Terry's little games. He stood still, hands clasped at groin height as if he might bow his head in prayer at any second.

"He has an extensive record in public service, beginning with his decorated career in the military, his dedication to local and state politics, and his election to Congress. You know the depth of his thought, the quality of his ideas. To that sterling brain he has added a full and generous heart. He is, in short, a man who belongs in the highest office in our land. Without further ado let me introduce you to the man behind Common 2 Cents, Congressman Sam Tompkins."

"What?" Amanda blurted out. The rest of the room seemed to have a similar response. Heads turned toward the back and after a few seconds Sam and his wife Charlene came down the center aisle. Charlene was doing her best to look First Ladyish. Sam beamed beside her and greeted a couple of the reporters as he moved past. To say the room was in shock might be a little too much, there were mostly reporters gathered there, after all, but the announcement had definitely caught them off guard.

Sam and Charlene reached the front row and Sam made a point of looking at both Amanda and Gary, gazing at them for a while, gauging their reaction it seemed, pleased perhaps to see both their chins scraping that lovely National Press Club carpet. Then he took the stage and a round of hugs among him, Caseworth, Terry and Charlene commenced as the shutter monster growled a few more times, growing even stronger as Sam took the microphones. He had prepared remarks and he pulled them from his suit coat pocket. He let the room settle.

Amanda had been riveted by her father's surprise presence, but now she looked over at Gary. He looked as if he were a six year-old and he'd just been told Santa didn't really exist. He couldn't have been more surprised or disillusioned. He was watching the death of his beautiful idea. He turned to Amanda and she thought he was either going to explode or burst into tears. She reached for his hand, grabbed the now-cold flesh and brought it into her lap. They had been hoodwinked, railroaded, and it was as if they were about to hear a jury's verdict. Amanda gave Gary's hand a squeeze but got no response. Sam cleared his throat and began.

"I apologize," he read. "I apologize for being so late to come forward and I want to begin by thanking Terry Rogers for her superb work in finding me and for convincing me to come here today. Terry, the country will always be in your debt."

He clapped his hands and the room followed tepidly.

"And I apologize to my wonderful daughter Amanda and to Gary King for keeping them in the dark so long, even about this news conference. Their dedication to this project, though at times unwitting, has been crucial to its success. I'm sure when the shock wears off they will understand why the secrecy was necessary. I hope you in the media give them their due accolades as you report on this chapter in our history.

"Now to the reason you and I are here. A politician's life is a full one and offers a person many avenues for expression in his or her work. But there are parts of political life, personal parts, that are not and should not be mixed in with that work. It was for this reason that I began posting my thoughts anonymously in Common 2 Cents. I have always been an admirer of Thomas Paine's monumental work at the founding of our country and I wanted to do as he did, publish my thoughts without taking personal credit for them, letting them simply become a part of the fabric of our society.

"I was happy to simply write and publish C2C and not worry about the numbers of readers. Worrying about numbers is integral to my work as a Congressman, but C2C afforded me a space in which I didn't have to have that concern. Then, in a coincidence I know many of you are going to find hard to believe was accidental, my daughter's friend, boyfriend, seized on C2C and turned the blog into the phenomenon you all know so well. I watched this happen and even was part of the wrangling over its consequences in my work with the DNC. But I didn't come forward.

"Why? Well, frankly, I agreed with Gary that the country needed to be able to first assess candidates by their thoughts, by the quality of their minds and hearts, before any messy personal details were known. Like most of you I didn't think much would happen with his call to arms. But, as you well know, something did happen, something huge and unprecedented in our history. The people truly spoke. After C2C's win in New Hampshire I was certain the air would run out of the balloon. Then, last week, when C2C was embraced by voters from both sides of the aisle, I was thrown into a deep quandary. I thought it was definitely time for C2C to come forward and I agreed with the DNC's rule that a candidate had to participate in the last debate, but I was reluctant to let the dream of a candidacy of ideas die. I thought maybe it would be best just to stay quiet.

"And then Terry found me, the jig was up, and I was relieved. I'm happy now to admit that I am in fact the author of the C2C blog and that I will gladly accept the delegates already pledged to C2C. I will begin campaigning immediately, but as far as a campaign committee and fundraising are concerned, things will continue as they have for the past two months. And I will not be using the C2C website to reach voters anymore. If anything appears on the site it will only mean some clever hacker has finally figured out my encryption.

"That's it for now. I'm very happy to have all this out in the open. On to Super Tuesday."

He folded up his prepared remarks and questions flew at him like bullets. The noise grew exponentially and Amanda, still holding Gary's hand, turned to him, pulled him closer and spoke into his ear over the din. It was an odd sensation, to have her warm breath in his ear as the cold noise of the room rose.

"Are you okay?" she asked.

"Yeah. But I'm sorry for you," Gary said.

"I'm sorry for him. What are you going to say?"

"I don't have to say anything."

They both sensed a presence nearby and saw four camera lenses circling them. They angled away.

"You've got to say something," Amanda said.

"He's your father," Gary said, playground style, with a smile.

"He's going to be your father-in-law, isn't he?"

Gary pulled back, surprised. "Wow. You said it."

Amanda smiled, but her mind was elsewhere. She looked at her father, at the scrum surrounding him, at her step-mother, and then back at Gary.

"Say something, Gary."

Amanda fastened him with a look he would know for the next fifty-three years of his life. A loving look but one that forced Gary to look inside himself and summon powers he didn't know he had. He stood. There was bedlam around him. Terry hadn't thought through the media hunger and was trying to deal with the flood of questions directed at Sam. Charlene was visibly rattled and started yelping words that didn't have any meaning. Gary waded through the crowd and made it to the stage. Charlene saw him and yelled at him to do something. He ignored her. He took a moment to watch the scene on the stage, the jostling and lenses and microphones all bouncing around. Messy democracy. But he could deal with it. He was married! He had a lifetime partner. He loved her. All this in front of him was a play. An interactive play. He went to Sam.

The route in was a gauntlet of microphones and faces and lenses and, at the end, Sam's smiling, expectant mug. Reporters sensed Gary's presence and opened a path for him. Sam spread his arms. Gary had the feeling he was walking into a malevolent embrace, about to get a spider's kiss. When they were close enough Gary and Sam put their hands on each other's shoulders, the cameras buzzed away, and a hug seemed just around the corner. But Gary resisted and soon the near embrace looked more like the beginning of a wrestling match than some sign of harmony. But Sam kept his cool and flashed the grin.

"Sorry, Gary," he said.

"Sorry for what? Sam. You've done everything right. Now you've got to keep going."

Sam tried again to bring Gary into a hug but couldn't. He turned to the reporters. "Did you get that?"

There was more buzzing and shouted questions until Gary raised his voice.

"And Sam! Sam!" The noise quieted. "And Sam, we're so relieved that you are the real C2C."

"Well, thank you, Gary. I..."

"And Sam, or as Amanda's cousins call you, Uncle Sam," that got a laugh, "We hope you put a quick stop to this C2C madness and get us back on track. You know I didn't want all this to happen. I was making a joke back then and so many people took me seriously. I mean, can you imagine walking into the Oval Office and saying something like, "Excuse me, President Blog?" I was worried that the real C2C might take me seriously as well, but those worries are over. We need you to re-establish order. We need you to get money back in the campaign. We need to forget about ideas and concentrate on the issues in the campaign, like who designs your suits, what cereal you like, what good friends you and your Mexican cleaning woman are. And if the people who supported C2C are disappointed by all this, well, to hell with them. They never understood where the power lies in Washington. Show 'em Sam. Show 'em what's what. Pull us back from the brink!"

Sam, who had been blinking heavily during this, trying to figure out what Gary was doing, once again went for a hug but Gary pulled back completely.

"And one other thing, Sam. Can I have your daughter's hand in marriage?"

Sam was startled. He turned to Amanda, standing now at her seat, and the room's eyes went to her. She gave her father a little wave and a smile, as if to say she was okay with the marriage proposal, but she didn't move toward him. Sam turned back to Gary.

"Of course you can," Sam said.

"Great," Gary said. He reached out, shook Sam's hand, turned, went to Amanda through the crush of reporters, she threw an arm around his shoulder and, brushing off all questions, they walked out of the stunned room.

16

Clips of Sam and Gary in their arm's-length embrace went viral and became the story of the revelation. Social media started to be quite unsocial when a deep division developed between those who interpreted the scene and Gary's speech as ironic and those who took it at face value, between those who believed Sam was the real C2C and those who didn't.

Gary went to the sidelines as this all developed and stayed there, telling reporters he'd already had his say, that the movement was now in Sam's hands. This was said with a wink that most reporters didn't get. Gary told Amanda, after one such misinterpretation, that the whole C2C phenomenon, from his dashed off essay to the present, was a stack of misinterpretations, ones, he admitted, he had sometimes engendered by his attempts to be truthful. Damned if you do, damned if you don't. He said the problem was trying to speak truth to power when power had no ears for such talk.

But while he wasn't doing much at all in the public eye as the days rolled toward Super Tuesday, as Sam took to the campaign trail with gusto, he was doing what he could to halt what he saw as the perversity of Sam's usurpation. He drove to Boston, met Ginny Evans at the airport and the two of them went to see Eve. She, of course, was incensed about Sam's entrance on the scene and was eager to do what she could to block him. The three spent a long weekend brainstorming, hanging out, and, for Ginny and Eve, falling more deeply in love.

The plan they hit upon was a simple one. They would shut down C2C, make sure everyone saw it was shut down, and hope that Sam would comment, say something about why he shut it down. Then they would put the site back up and force him to make another comment. He would of course say that he had been hacked but that would occasion those who were asking him to open the encryption to redouble their efforts. In the end, they hoped, the website would act like a boa constrictor and suffocate Sam's campaign.

It took two off-on cycles for the website to begin to do just that. All reporters seemed to want to know about was why the damn thing kept blinking on and off. They challenged Sam to show them he was truly in control of the technology, to predict when it would turn off or on. Sam dodged that challenge at every turn but it was clear he was getting nervous. His phone calls to Amanda were bouncy and dissembling, but the subtext was that things weren't going well. The C2C "brand" plummeted in the polls and Sam struggled to keep his nose above water. His demise came into view on the horizon when he said that his campaign would need donations to keep going. His first public donor, with an in-kind offer of use of a private jet, was none other than the walking punch line, Donald Trump.

Gary was offered scads to write a book but he declined all requests. He told agents and editors that it was too early, that he and the country needed to see what would come of the upheaval he had inadvertently excited. Terry Rogers, on the other hand, gladly took a million dollar advance for her story of the scales falling from her eyes and her dogged investigation. But the deal looked to be fraught when one of the first headlines about the book sale read, "Terra Firma's Account Goes For One Million, To Be Shelved in Fiction or Non-Fiction?"

Amanda and Gary spent a little while after their on-camera

engagement wondering if they'd been too hasty, too caught up in the moment. Amanda walked out of one dinner crying after Gary had said he wished their vows of commitment had come more "organically." They patched that up later that night but by then a smartphone video of Amanda leaving the restaurant had gone viral.

On the Friday before Super Tuesday, in Los Angeles, Sam, hounded by reporters asking about yet another instance of the C2C website going on and off, lost his cool and shouted nonsense about computers and technology and ended his rant with what sounded like a military commander telling reporters to "stand down." Unable to get anything more out of him the reporters turned to Terry Rogers who said she couldn't comment due to her pending book deal. The media jumped on that one-two burst of political incompetence and rode it all weekend. By Monday morning Sam's claim to be C2C was in serious jeopardy and C2C supporters were in open revolt against Sam's candidacy.

Gary called Eve about eleven-thirty that morning and they both agreed it was time to shut down C2C for good.

"Would you have done it all over again if you knew how things would turn out?" Gary asked.

"I don't know. You?" Eve said.

"You got a girlfriend out of the whole thing."

"You got a wife."

"Not yet."

"I don't think I'd do it again," Eve said. "Don't tell Ginny that. But what was I thinking invading someone's privacy?"

"That people needed to hear what he was saying. Are you ever going to tell me his name?"

"No. That's my secret forever."

"I'm not sure I'd do it again either," Gary said. It's all been too ad hoc. I still believe we need to make our decisions on something other than personalities, but it was all so helter-skelter the way it rolled out for C2C."

Gary and Amanda flew out to Los Angeles that afternoon for

a reunion of the brain trust at Ed Popper's house. They were going to watch the returns and weren't worried about a thousand C2C supporters showing up on Ed's modest front yard. Gary requested that the menu for the night include a Subway turkey club sandwich. "I'll keep it down this time," he told Ed.

After hanging up with Gary, Eve went to the computer at Halligan Hall and wrote a final, one word, ironic post. "CULater." She stared at that for a few minutes, saw that the hits were starting to build exponentially, as they always did with a new post, and then she dismantled the whole website. She spent an hour checking every deletion, calling Ginny to tell her what she was doing and to make sure there were no mistakes. Late in the afternoon it was done. C2C was no more.

She went back to her unit at the hospital and as she passed a waiting room she saw a television with Sam's agitated face filling the frame. She stood and watched for a while as he fulminated, lashed out at reporters, and tried to stay somewhat calm. Then Eve heard some laughter from the hallway and looked to see three white-coated doctors and one in casual clothes sharing some kind of joke. She was about to look away when she realized Adam was the doctor in casual wear. Their paths hadn't crossed in months and Eve wasn't certain that if she went up to him he would remember her. She kept one eye on the waiting room television and one on the knot of doctors. It broke up after a while and Adam started walking toward her. Eve wondered if it was really him or if she had just conjured him after seeing Sam on the news. As Adam got closer though she realized he was real and that he was looking at her. She smiled, expecting one of those colleague nods you got all the time in the hospital. But he slowed as he neared.

"Hi Eve," he said.

Eve turned to him. "Hi. You remembered my name."

"How could Adam forget Eve, huh?"

They laughed and Eve suddenly remembered why it was she had invaded his privacy. There was something about being in his presence that made her feel more herself. She couldn't explain it scientifically. It wasn't attraction to him in any conventional sense. It might have been the way he carried himself or his smile or the simple fact that he seemed so at ease he made others feel at ease with themselves. But it didn't matter why it happened, just that it did happen, she had experienced it, and she had tried to share her experience with the world.

"Congratulations," Eve said. "I hear you have a granddaughter."

Adam gave her a long look and Eve realized she had spoken without thinking.

"How did you know? Was there some kind of announcement?"

"I'm, uh, not sure. I guess I heard it around somewhere. You're a popular guy."

For a moment Eve couldn't tell from Adam's look if he suspected something, but soon his grin appeared.

"We get to see her in person tomorrow. Polly, that's her name, is pretty photogenic but we're looking forward to seeing her in person."

"That'll be nice."

Adam nodded but something else was occupying him. He looked at Eve for a long time, then spoke.

"Are you good at keeping secrets?" he asked.

"Yeah, I think so."

"I need to confess. If I confessed to you would you promise to keep it between us?"

"Scout's honor."

"My daughter lives in Buffalo. Her mother died giving birth to her and as the date of my granddaughter's birth approached I couldn't shake the feeling that something bad was going to happen to Hannah, my daughter. I didn't tell her anything like that, of course. And I drove out to Buffalo for the birth, stayed in a motel, and pretended to my daughter I was still here, in Boston. After Polly was born my daughter asked that Michelle and I not come out for a couple of weeks, so I couldn't tell her where I was. But I did go up and see my granddaughter before I left. Isn't that screwy."

"No, that's beautiful."

"It was in a way. But I'm still embarrassed about it, so lips sealed, huh?"

Eve felt tears welling and didn't know if Adam would understand the depth of her feeling.

"Lips sealed," she managed to get out.

A voice rose from the waiting room, the deep biting voice of a patient talking to another patient, gesturing toward Sam's face on television.

"He ain't the real one. He's just catchin' on the coattails. Ain't nobody should vote his ass for nothin'."

There was agreement among the others in the waiting room. Adam and Eve had been drawn to this voice and now turned back to each other.

"Do you think that's right?" Eve said. Then she realized that he may know he was the real C2C, that all the publicity had to have put the blog in front of him.

"About this C2C? I don't know anything much about it. Haven't followed it, really, although you can't get away from it. My wife's a fan, though. She actually went up to New Hampshire when they had the primary there. I was away pretending not to be in Buffalo. She's not too happy about this guy."

"I liked his blog very much."

"Michelle says I sound like him, some of the things he says. She showed me one of his posts that was almost word for word like an email I'd sent her. She thinks I was hacked." He chuckled. "That would be something, wouldn't it?"

"Maybe you should write a blog yourself."

Adam smiled. "No, I don't think the world needs my two cents. I've got another idea I'm working on."

"Oh? What?"

"Nothing much, really. I'm going to keep it to myself for now. I don't think it would have much interest for others."

"Who knows? Look at what happened to C2C."

Another smile from Adam. "Despite what Michelle says, I'm no C2C," he said. "Gotta run. Good seeing you."

He put a soft hand on her shoulder instead of a handshake, turned and walked down the hall. That man, she thought, could have been the next president of the United States. But he was above that and she was glad her effort to bring him to the public had turned out the way it did. She did wonder about this new idea of his and thought maybe she should reopen the channels into his world. But she quickly rejected that. She had learned her lesson. She was happy just to know him.

She turned back to the turbulence of the television images. The scene changed to Gary and Amanda caught by reporters coming off a plane, both of them waving off questions. Then a reporter shouted out a question that stopped them.

"When are you going to run for office, Gary?"

"I'm going to run for office when the vast majority of the people in this country, the ninety-nine percent, hold the power and the money-lenders have been driven out of the temple. In other words, not in my lifetime."

Eve couldn't make out much on the screen. Her vision was distorted by her tears of joy. She started to wipe them away, but then just let them come. She didn't need to see all that. She, like the rest of the country, had seen enough.

ACKNOWLEDGEMENTS

Many thanks to the following for their help with my virgin self-publishing adventure: Linda Esposito, Mary Hedahl, Pat Arnow, Julie Trelstad, Ashley Gorham, Julie Smith, Stacey Weaver, David Guaspari, Jeany Wolf, Bill Tate, Kit Foster, Ryan Zee, Ann Rittenberg and Dan Weiss. I'm sure there will be more as the book makes its way in the world. I thank you all in advance.